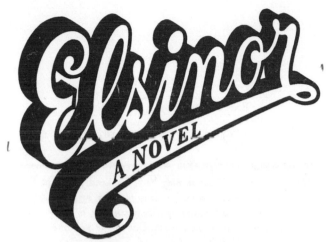

Elsinor

A NOVEL

CHARLES WEBB

McGraw-Hill Book Company

New York   St. Louis   San Francisco
Toronto   Mexico   Düsseldorf

Book design by Lynn Braswell.

1 2 3 4 5 6 7 8 9 BPBP 7 9 8 7 6

Library of Congress Cataloging in Publication Data

Webb, Charles Richard, date
Elsinor.

I. Title.
PZ4.W364El   [PS3573.E195]   813'.5'4   76-20804
ISBN 0-07-068803-6

to

Joyce

&

Elaine

$\mathcal{T}$WO TORCHES, flickering in a light rain, stood at either side of the entrance to the Blue Stallion Baths as Laura Foster walked up to the building and pulled a large handle on the door. When it didn't open, she took hold of a brass knocker, made in the shape of a rearing horse, and banged it down several times.

The door opened inward several inches and the face of a man appeared.

"I'm trying to locate someone," Laura said.

The man glanced down the sidewalk, then back at her. "I can't disturb the guests." He began closing the door but she put her hand around the edge of it.

Another face appeared, gray hair combed down over a forehead. "What is it."

"She wants to locate someone."

"I'm trying to find John Foster. I phoned, but they wouldn't get him."

"Go put some fresh towels in the disco room, Terence. I'll handle this." The second man turned back to Laura. "Come in a minute."

Laura stepped through the door. A black man

seated behind a desk across the room glanced up at her.

The man who'd let her in was holding out his hand. "Your coat's dripping."

"If you could just tell him I'm out here," she said as she removed it. "It's very important." She handed it to him.

"John Foster," he said, looking down at several drops of water that had fallen onto the thick carpet.

"Yes."

"I don't know him." He turned the hem of the coat up so it didn't drip. "Mrs. Foster, by any chance?"

"Yes."

"Mrs. Foster, do you know about our club?"

"Yes."

He nodded. "Well, so you see, we really couldn't bother him. No. What I suggest you do is walk back down to the boulevard where there's an all-night drug store. Purchase an umbrella and return. Station yourself across the street. Your husband can come out no other way but by the front door. And when he does, Mrs. Foster, walk right up and greet him." He smiled. "It's been my pleasure. I'm needed inside now."

The man behind the desk cleared his throat. "Mr. Spencer?"

"Yes, Mark."

"I took the call when she phoned in, and when I wouldn't get him for her she threatened to go to the police."

"You told me to file a missing person's report," Laura said.

"Please, please," Mr. Spencer said, raising his hand. "Mrs. Foster." He rested his fingers lightly on her wrist.

"You wait here. I'll go in and see if I can find him."

"Oh, thank you."

He turned around and pushed open a door in a red velveteen wall.

Mark folded his hands on the desk, looked down at them, and began humming softly.

"Excuse me," Laura said.

Pursing his lips slightly, he continued to hum.

"Excuse me? Would you mind if I looked at the register?"

He looked up.

"I noticed a register. Would you mind if I took a quick look at it?"

The man looked down at a book of signatures in front of him, then back at Laura. "Yes."

"You'd mind."

"Of course."

Laura seated herself on a small settee and raised her eyes to the picture over his head of a wild blue horse painted on black velvet.

When Mr. Spencer came back through the door he was shaking his head. "I'm sorry," he said.

"You didn't find him."

He pushed the door closed.

"You didn't find John."

"Obviously he didn't find him," Mark said. "Mr. Spencer, she asked me to show her the register."

"If I could just glance at it a moment I could see if he signed in."

"And what if he didn't use his real name?" Mark said.

"I know his handwriting."

"Show it to her," Mr. Spencer said.

Laura went to the desk and bent over the book. She ran her finger down the columns of names until she reached the middle of the second page. "Here."

Mr. Spencer bent forward.

"John Kelly." She looked up at him.

"What about him."

"It's my husband's writing."

Mr. Spencer looked at the name. "It's John Kelly's writing."

Laura straightened up and turned to face him. "Mr. Spencer, my seeing John now will make the difference between our staying married or not. Does that matter to you?"

"Certainly."

"That's not an exaggeration. It was very hard for me to come here."

He nodded.

"And it's not easy to stand here like this," she said.

"May I ask if you have children, Mrs. Foster."

"Two."

Mark made a loud sniffling noise. "Did you see my hanky, Mr. Spencer?"

She pointed at the door beside them. "Let me go look for him myself."

"I can't do that."

"Very quickly. I won't disturb the guests."

"What are the names of your two children, Mrs. Foster."

"Flora and Tom."

"Mrs. Foster," he said, pushing his hands down into his pockets, "you judge me harshly."

"I don't judge you at all. You just weren't in there long enough to look everywhere for him."

"You'd be hard put to find a more devoted friend of the American family than I, Mrs. Foster."

"Then let me go look for him."

"But how do I know you're not trifling with me, just to get a look inside."

"Sir, I don't care what goes on in your establishment, I'm here because I want my husband."

"Sobeit." He glanced at Mark. "Get out the closet key."

"Mr. Spencer."

"Do as I say." He turned back to Laura. "I'm a generous man, Mrs. Foster. Generous to a fault, I'm told. But quick, also, to wrath."

"I'm not trifling with you, Mr. Spencer."

The assistant rummaged through a desk drawer.

Mr. Spencer reached down and took Laura's hand. "Don't judge me, dear girl."

"No."

"The key's not here."

"Try the bottom drawer."

Mark pushed closed the drawer in which he'd been looking and pulled open the one below it.

"Don't hold me insensitive to your need because of the difference between us."

"I don't."

Holding the key, Mark got up from his desk.

"My helper will accompany you into the closet,"

Mr. Spencer said. "Put a few things on so you won't stand out."

"Put what on."

"Mark will show you," he said. "Do you have any tissues with you?"

"Yes."

"Wipe your lipstick off before you return. I'll accompany you inside when you're ready."

"You want me to change my clothes?"

"Just go with Mark, Mrs. Foster."

Laura watched as Mark inserted his key into the lock of a door behind the desk.

"Why couldn't I just go in like this."

"Mrs. Foster."

Mark pulled open the door, then reached inside to turn on the light. "Are you coming?"

Laura looked into a large closet where clothes hung from hooks on the wall. "You want me to dress up like a man?"

"I have to think of my membership, Mrs. Foster."

"But that's what you want me to do."

Mr. Spencer glanced up at the ceiling.

"I just wasn't sure if that's what you were asking."

Mr. Spencer smiled.

Laura walked into the closet and looked at a pile of clothing in one of the corners. Mark came in after her. "I'm going to shut the door," he said, closing it, "but don't panic, honey."

Laura glanced at a rumpled athletic supporter on a shelf at the far side of the room, then at the clothing on the floor. She walked to it, reached down and pulled up a blue turtleneck sweater by one of its arms.

"That's not your size." Mark pushed several hangers along a bar running across the room, then removed one with a brown suit on it. "Wear this." He handed it to her, then bent down and pulled up a white shirt from the pile of clothing. "Here." At the far end of the bar hung several neckties. He pulled down a green one and gave it to her.

Laura looked at the clothing over her arm.

"I suppose you're going to tell me it's not you."

"I just don't see why all this is necessary."

"Look," Mark said, keeping his eyes fixed on hers. "Mr. Spencer's going way out on a limb to do this. Just don't push him any further."

"I wasn't trying to."

Mark turned around and faced the wall. Laura looked a moment at the back of his head, then bent over and set the clothing down on the floor. She reached behind herself for the buttons of her dress, undid them, then stepped out of it. She rested it over the bar, picked up the pants and pushed her legs into them.

"I know whose suit that is, by the way, and I don't think he'd appreciate this, so I suggest you try not to rumple it."

She pulled the pants up around her waist, snapped them and zipped the fly. "I need a belt."

He pulled a wide black belt from the clothing pile and handed it to her without turning around.

Laura fitted it through the loops of her pants and buckled it. She put one of her arms into a shirtsleeve.

"Tuck that in when you're finished," Mark said, turning around. "And the jacket goes on next."

"I know." She finished putting on the shirt, then slipped her arms through the sleeves of the jacket.

"Do you know how to tie a tie?"

"I think so."

"In other words you don't." He removed the tie from her hand, stepped up to her and ran it under the collar of the shirt. Quickly, he looped one end around the other, made a knot, and cinched it up under her neck. "Don't shove your boobies around at everybody inside either." He stepped back to look at the knot. "And I want you to wear a cap." He lifted down a white visored cap from the shelf.

"I guess you don't think this all looks just a little strange."

"Put your hair up on your head. I don't want it showing."

Laura opened her purse and reached inside. She brought out two bobby pins, piled her hair up on her head, fastened one pin into it, and then the other. She took the cap from his hand and put it on.

"Tight."

"It's tight." She reached into her purse for a piece of Kleenex and wiped several times at her lips. "I'm ready."

Mark opened the door and pointed for her to go out. He turned off the light and followed. "The cap was my idea," he said to Mr. Spencer, who rose from a settee as they came in. "Her hair has a peculiar texture and I think it's best covered."

"Shall we go in?" Mr. Spencer said.

"Thank you."

They stepped forward to the door leading inside. "You will, of course, pay my club the respect it is due."

Laura nodded, looking down at the handle of the door.

"You do appreciate what I'm doing for you."

"I want to find my husband, Mr. Spencer. I appreciate what you're doing."

"Mark," Mr. Spencer said, nodding toward the coatrack in the corner, "roll up Mrs. Foster's mackintosh and put it under the desk till we come out." He pulled open the velveteen door.

Laura stepped through.

"We needn't speak in here," Mr. Spencer said, following her, holding apart the curtain in front of them, "just look till you find him, and don't take any unnecessary time." He pointed at the small pool, bright orange lights shining up through the water. The darkened forms of two men swimming side by side moved slowly down its length.

Laura took several steps toward the pool, leaned forward slightly to study them, then walked back and shook her head.

"No?"

She looked past the pool at the small snack bar. Three men, each with a white towel wrapped around his waist, sat on stools in front of the counter. Laura watched a boy set a paper plate of french-fried potatoes down in front of one of them. "May we get a little closer to the eating place," she said.

"You see him."

"I can't tell." She squinted at the back of the man on the end stool. "I just want to go closer."

Mr. Spencer led her forward along a wet rubber runner beside the pool. As they approached the snack bar he took her arm and moved her over beside a small palm tree rising from a round pottery urn. "I would rather not get closer than this."

"He's facing the other way," she said.

Holding hands, two young men walked past them and into a hallway on the other side of a second potted palm. Laura watched them disappear, then looked back at the man on the stool. "I'll just walk a little bit forward, so I can see his profile." She took several steps, and looked at the man's face. His elbows on the counter, he was picking his teeth with a toothpick. She returned to Mr. Spencer, shaking her head.

He pointed across the room. "I'll explain why the lights are kept so dim," he said as they started around the other end of the pool.

Laura glanced down at a man seated in a low round chair, his towel fallen beside him, his legs slowly opening and closing.

"Mrs. Foster?"

"Why the lights are dim," she said, "yes, I'd be interested to know."

"Not because we're ashamed of what we do here," he said quietly. "But because we, too, possess qualities of allurement and charm."

Laura nodded.

"You understand me."

"Allurement and charm."

They walked up several wooden stairs together. At the top was a narrow window. At one side of it a man, towel around his waist, was bent forward, his hands cupped beside his face as he peered through the glass.

"This is a view into the steam room. We'll leave no stone unturned." He rubbed his hand across the window in front of them to clear away a layer of moisture.

"May I look in?"

"Yes, Mrs. Foster."

Laura bent forward and looked through the glass into a large room. Its walls were decorated with patterns made of small white and blue tiles. Seated on a mosaic bench across from her two naked men were talking. Beside them stood another, running his fingers through his hair. A man walked past the window and when he'd gone by Laura moved to the glass and looked through the steam to the far end of the room where two men were standing, very close, pressing together.

"Do you see him?"

She stepped back from the window.

"Did you?"

"Mr. Spencer, there must be some way to page him. A brief announcement asking him to come to the front desk is all it would take."

"He's not in there."

"No."

"Let's move on."

Laura glanced at the man at the other end of the platform, then followed Mr. Spencer back down the stairs.

At the bottom he raised his arm toward the hallway

where the two young men had gone, its entrance glowing red from the colored lightbulbs overhead and inside. "No, charm and grace are not qualities restricted to the so-called fair sex alone, Mrs. Foster."

A bald man dove into the pool beside her and Laura walked after Mr. Spencer toward the glowing hall. From a loudspeaker above came a melody of violins. "I really think if you have a loudspeaker for music you could very easily use it to page John."

"Patience, Mrs. Foster. One of the three great virtues." They reached the hallway as a tall nude man walked out holding a comb.

"Mr. Spencer."

"We're here to search for your husband, Mrs. Foster."

"But you could page him."

"You *do* want to find him." He frowned slightly. "You *are* serious about this."

She looked into the tunnel before them. Stretching back was a long row of blue doors, some closed, others partly open. "What's all this now," she said.

"After you, Mrs. Foster."

"What is it."

"Just rooms."

"What for."

"Mrs. Foster," he said, softly clearing his throat, "you told me you were familiar with our purposes here."

"I just asked you what the rooms were for."

"The relaxation of our guests."

She looked down the hall a moment longer, then walked forward, slowly, passing two closed doors, then coming to one which was ajar. Inside was the glow of a cigarette.

"Try not to be conspicuous, Mrs. Foster."

"John doesn't smoke."

"Excuse me?"

"He doesn't smoke. That wouldn't be him."

"Oh." Mr. Spencer extended his arm for her to continue. She glanced down toward the end of the hallway.

"Anything wrong?"

"I'm not going to be able to find him in here."

"Perseverance, Mrs. Foster."

"Can't you *please* page him for me?" she said, turning to him.

"I truly wish I could."

"Oh God," a man's voice said from the other side of a closed door.

Laura turned toward the door.

"Oh God," he said more loudly.

"Is that your husband's voice?"

She continued looking at the door. "No."

"Move along, Mrs. Foster."

She walked past another of the closed doors. "I want to go back, Mr. Spencer."

"There. Is that him?"

At the end of the hall stood a man in a towel. A large erection rose up beneath the white material.

"Mr. Spencer." She turned toward him again.

"Not him."

"No, Mr. Spencer."

"Around the turn in the hall there," he said, "we'll come to what's known as the Roustabout Room. You may very, very likely find him there. New members and guests here for the first or second time often congregate in the Roustabout Room, where many lasting friendships have formed over the years. Congeniality is the rule."

"This is ridiculous." The man in the towel smiled at her as she approached. She kept her eyes fixed on a point past him on the wall, then turned as the hallway came to a corner.

Mr. Spencer stepped ahead of her and pulled aside a curtain that covered a wide doorway.

"This is the Roustabout Room?"

"The very same."

Laura looked into it. "It's pitch dark. How can I see him in there."

"You'll sense his presence, if he's here."

Laura looked back at him a moment, then stepped into the room. He came after her, letting the curtain fall back over the doorway.

On the other side of the room someone groaned.

"Do you feel his nearness," Mr. Spencer whispered, his face close to hers.

Beside her was a wet, slapping noise.

Laura reached behind her and threw back the curtain. "Mr. Spencer," she said, stepping out of the room, "are you enjoying all this?"

The door beside them was open. Laura turned to see a man on his hands and knees on the floor behind another man. "Oh no," she said.

Mr. Spencer stepped out of the Roustabout Room beside her. "Mrs. Foster, your cap's slipping off."

Laura reached up and pulled off the cap.

The man kneeling inside the small room glanced out at her, then reached over and closed the door.

"You go page John on the intercom, Mr. Spencer, or you're going to have a scene in here that you will not believe."

From the other end of the hallway the man in the towel had come several steps closer to them to look at Laura. His erection drooped partway down toward his knee.

"Come with me now, Mrs. Foster." He took her elbow, but she pulled away.

"John!"

"Now see here."

"John Foster!"

The face of a red-haired man appeared through the curtain beside them.

"I'm looking for my husband, John Foster," Laura said to him.

Another door opened along the hallway and a man stepped out holding his penis.

"Are you here, John?"

"Everyone back inside," Mr. Spencer said, holding up his arms as another door opened. "It's under control."

"John, if you *can* hear me, please answer!"

Mr. Spencer went to the man holding his penis. "It's nothing," he said, easing him into his room again.

"John Foster!"

"I'll call him," Mr. Spencer said. He cleared his throat and turned toward the open doorways. "We're looking for a Mr. John Foster. Is he here? John Foster."

"He just left," said the man who was looking out of the Roustabout Room.

"You know him," Laura said.

Mr. Spencer hurried to where they were standing. "You know John Foster."

"Will you come with us to the office," Mr. Spencer said. "As you can see, this woman's terribly upset."

"What does he look like," Laura said. "I want to be sure."

He shrugged.

"Tell her what he looks like."

"Six feet or so. Brown hair. Glasses."

"That's him."

Mr. Spencer held open the curtain. "Could we go to the office."

"Whom did he leave with," Laura said.

The man looked back into the room. "Who was Foster with?"

One of the men inside said something, and several others laughed.

"He's my husband, he's left me, if you know anything at all, please help me."

There was no answer from the dark room.

The first man glanced at Laura, then back at Mr. Spencer. "She says this is urgent."

"*Very*," Laura said.

Mr. Spencer nodded.

"There's an outside chance I have the name of the fellow he's with at my apartment." He looked up at Laura's face for a moment. "I'd have to be sure it was important."

"Children," Mr. Spencer said, "all that."

The man began getting up.

"Oh thank you," Laura said, stepping back so he could come out of the room. She reached up to wipe the perspiration off her forehead. "Thank you. Thank you. Thank you."

She thanked him several more times as he drove to his apartment. When they got there she followed him up a narrow flight of stairs to a door, which he unlocked with a key from a chain in his pocket.

"May I ask your name?"

"Paul." He walked through ahead of her, and went to a table where there was an address book. He picked it up and turned through it until he reached one of the pages near the middle, then bent the book back and dialed a number.

"Is that who he's with?" Laura said.

He glanced over at her.

"Did you find the name of the person John's with?"

"I don't have the name. I'm calling someone who can tell me." After holding the receiver to his ear for several moments, he returned it to the phone.

"You didn't wait very long."

He walked past her to close the door. "It was busy."

"Well then he's there, your friend's there."

"I've wanted to say something," he said, returning across the room, "and I think I should, because I don't want to pretend." He reached down to smooth the corner of a small throw rug beside his foot. "It's against my principles to help anyone who feels superior to me, but I'm doing it this time because you're so desperate."

She watched him straighten up. "I don't feel superior to you."

Paul walked to a cupboard, opened it and removed an iron. He carried it to the table and pushed the telephone aside. "Can you hand me that towel?"

Folded on the seat of a chair beside her was a large towel. Laura picked it up and handed it to him.

"I guess it doesn't seem that way to you, it's so ingrained." He opened the towel till it covered most of the table. "Would you like a glass of sherry?"

"I don't need anything."

After plugging the end of the cord of the iron into a wall socket, Paul reached into an open closet beside him for a pair of light-colored pants and laid them flat on the towel. "I'll try Lee again in a few minutes." She watched him smooth the legs flat, then lift the iron and rest it on a cuff. He ran it slowly up the leg, then back down.

"What if I tried calling him myself," Laura said. "To save you the trouble."

The iron stopped. Paul looked down at the piece of clothing. "I don't think I know your name."

"Laura."

"If you'd like to go home now," he said, "I'll give you cab fare and you can wait in the hall till the taxi comes."

She stood looking at his hand on the iron. "Why would I want to go home."

He lifted the iron up slightly from the cloth and turned around. "This is my apartment."

"I know."

"I don't know anything about you or your husband."

"Well we were getting ready to go away for the weekend and he disappeared."

"But that doesn't entitle you to come here and start using my phone. I offered you a glass of sherry to help calm yourself and you turned it down."

"Where is it."

"In the kitchen."

Laura walked across the room and through the entranceway of the kitchen, looking back at him from the other room.

"On the shelf." He pointed through the doorway, then lifted the phone and dialed again. He stood listening a moment before speaking. "Lee?" he said. Again he listened, then hung up.

Laura stepped to the doorway, holding a bottle by its neck.

"Lee couldn't talk just now. He'll call me back in a minute. There's a glass in there on the shelf."

When she returned Laura was carrying a small glass of pale liquid. She took it to a chair and sat, watched him iron a few moments as she sipped from the glass. "I know you don't like me to talk, but I want to know if your friend said anything more than that he'd call back."

"Why do you say I don't want you to talk."

"Because you're busy."

He moved the appliance slowly up toward the pocket. "I hope my IQ level isn't so low I can't concentrate on ironing a pair of pants if someone's speaking to me."

She watched him reach down and tug slightly at the end of the leg to straighten it. "I guess he didn't say anything more than that he'd call back," she said.

Paul unplugged the iron and wound the cord around the handle as Laura set her empty glass on the floor. "Help yourself to more."

"That was enough."

He folded the towel. Laura watched as he carried it to a bureau at the foot of his bed, opened a drawer and put it inside.

"When you said it was against your principles to help someone who felt superior to you," she said, "I guess you thought I felt that way about you because you're a homosexual."

He pushed the drawer closed.

"But I don't, if it's what you were thinking."

He stood with his eyes on a yellow hairbrush till the phone rang, then walked quickly past her and picked it up. "Lee?" He turned away from her. "Who was Foster with tonight?"

Laura moved forward on the chair.

"Do you know where?" Paul said. He nodded. "Thank you." He hung up the phone.

Laura got up. "What," she said.

"They stopped by Lee's earlier, but they're gone now."

"They were with Lee?"

"That's what he said, but not now."

"But you didn't ask any questions. Why didn't you?"

"Because there was nothing else to find out. They left the club together and went to Lee's. Then they left Lee's and he doesn't know where they went."

"But he must have said more than that."

Paul walked to the chair where she'd been sitting,

bent down and picked up the empty glass from the floor.

"Why did you just say goodbye," Laura said. "Can I please call him back?"

"He wouldn't talk to you."

She hurried in front of him and stood between him and the doorway to the kitchen. "Will you please tell me what's happening?"

"I have."

"You keep giving me part of it," she said. "I have to know how to find John."

"I'm sorry but he'd left Lee's house when Lee called," he said, looking down at the glass. "If I could have prevented his leaving I would have, but I couldn't."

"He was probably there the first time you talked to Lee, when Lee said he'd call back."

"He may have been."

"If you could just have said then that you wanted John, he probably would have gotten him."

Paul looked past her into the kitchen.

"And then when he called back you didn't ask him anything. Don't you understand? John's my husband."

"I thought I could help you, and it turned out I couldn't."

"You didn't try to get any information from him," she said. "Can't you at least tell me something about who John's with? If you know who it is?"

"He's with Elsinor." He carried the empty glass toward the kitchen.

"Who?"

"Look."

"Elsinor? That's the name of the person he's with?"

"That's who it is."

She followed him across the room. "Well is that his first name or his last?"

"It's his full name. May I put the glass in the kitchen?"

She stepped out of his way.

He carried it in and set it down on the shelf. For a few moments he stood with his hand around it, then walked back into the other room. "Your husband doesn't seem to wish to be with you. I don't know his reasons, but he seems to feel strongly about his reasons and I think you'd better respect them."

"I can't respect them if I don't know what they are."

"Would you be interested to hear what little I know about Elsinor."

"Please."

"He doesn't live around here," Paul said, frowning slightly. "I believe he stays at hotels, or the club. I don't know where he comes from. He travels a lot. He doesn't really have friends. I think he has something to do with ships. I'm not sure, though. And that's all I know." He turned and walked back toward the front of the room.

"What if I did this," Laura said. "Just called Lee back very quickly and asked him if he knew what hotel Elsinor's staying in."

Paul went to the side of the large window overlooking the street and pulled closed a heavy curtain. "He wouldn't tell you even if he knew."

"Why not."

"If *I* called him back to ask where Elsinor was staying, with Lee knowing you were looking for the person

Elsinor was with, he'd hang up on *me*." He walked to the other side of the window. "First thing in the morning I have to leave for Santa Barbara. I'm sorry I wasn't more help, but I've done all I can." He jiggled the material in the center of the curtain where it had caught on the sill.

"My parents are expecting a call from me," Laura said.

Paul walked to a table beside the bed and picked up a white alarm clock.

"I took the children to my parents' before we were supposed to leave on our trip. It was when I got home that John wasn't there."

"Where were you going?"

"Lake Tahoe."

Paul turned the knob on the back of the clock.

"We would have gotten up there by now. They must be wondering why I haven't called."

He set the clock on the table. "Call them from here if you must."

"And say what," she said, looking at the telephone.

"Tell them you got there." After seating himself on the bed, he reached down to remove one of his shoes, took a small bottle of black shoe polish off the table and unscrewed its top.

"I can't do that."

"Then don't tell them anything and let them assume you got there." He dabbed some fluid onto the toe of his shoe with an applicator extending down from the cap. "Or do you want them to sit up and worry all night that you were killed."

Laura watched him blow on the end of his shoe,

then picked up the phone. She dialed, and listened into the receiver. "Mother?" she said finally. "We're just exhausted, both of us. I just want you to tell Tommy and Flora we miss and love them and we'll see them Sunday." She listened into the phone, then frowned. "Who?" she said.

Paul rubbed polish on the back of his shoe.

"When," Laura said. She looked down at the table. "Okay, mom, we're thinking of you too." She slowly lowered the receiver. "Someone called for me."

Paul rested his shoe on the floor.

"Someone's trying to reach me. A man."

"Who."

"He called several times, but didn't leave his name." She turned toward Paul. "This has something to do with John. Please may I call my house, just in case John went back there."

"This will be your last call."

She lifted the receiver again, dialed, and listened as the phone rang in her own house.

"I take it your parents would have recognized your husband's voice if it was him."

"It wasn't." The phone rang several more times, then slowly she replaced the receiver.

Paul had fitted the second shoe over his hand. He pushed the applicator down into the bottle of polish and lifted it out.

"You mentioned you were leaving in the morning for Santa Barbara."

"That's right."

"May I ask how long you'll be up there?"

"A day and a half." He carefully ran the applicator around the edge of the sole.

"Are you visiting someone up there?"

"May I know why you're asking this?" He looked up.

"I have to do something till Sunday, Paul. I don't want to sit in an empty house and go crazy."

"You aren't suggesting you come with me."

"Paul, my children aren't at home. John's gone. I don't know what to do. I don't understand about his going to those baths. Maybe I could at least understand something about that if you'd let me talk to you just a little more about it."

"Don't you have friends you can go to?"

"I don't want to get anyone involved in this till I know what it is."

He lowered the shoe. "I suppose you don't think you're involving me."

"Yes, Paul, I'm involving you, and I'm sorry, but I just can't go home and sit waiting by the phone for two days. This has never happened to me before. I will do everything in my power not to bother you. I will ride up in the back of your car tomorrow and you won't even know I'm there. But I just don't want to be alone right now. Is that impossible to understand?"

He looked back at the shoe. "How can I do my work up there if you're with me."

"You'll see that I won't get in your way, Paul." She put her hand on the arm of an overstuffed chair beside her. "I'd like to push this into the next room and sleep in it tonight."

"Are you really serious."

"May I, Paul. *Please?*"

He rested his hand with the shoe on it beside him on the blanket. "I just want to know if you're actually serious."

"Thank you, Paul." She pushed the chair across the floor and into the kitchen.

$\mathcal{L}$AURA was up an hour before Paul. She stood at a window beside the refrigerator looking down at the street until the alarm went off.

Paul didn't talk to her as he got up, but washed his face, removed the pants he'd ironed the night before from the closet and put them on. For several minutes he knelt beside his bureau removing small boxes and a camera from a drawer and fitting them into a canvas bag. When he was finished he went to the kitchen, emptied a packet of pink powder into a glass, filled the glass with milk and drank it.

Laura waited in the hall as he locked his door, then walked down the stairs behind him. She climbed into the back seat of the car, where she sat looking out her window as Paul drove to Santa Barbara.

The house where Paul was going was at the end of a street, up on a hill behind the city. At the bottom of the driveway were two tall iron gates, closed, and beside them a metal box on a pipe. When they reached it Paul stopped the car and rolled down his window. He spoke into the box, giving his name, and a moment later the gates swung slowly open, so he could drive through.

At the top of the driveway, surrounded by eucalyptus trees, was a parking circle. Paul parked and got out, but instead of walking up to the house he bent over and opened his bag. He reached inside for a lens, held it up and looked through it at the large front porch. Laura watched through the window of the car as he took out a notebook, quickly wrote something in it, then returned it and closed the bag. She pushed the seat forward and opened the door as he started toward the house, but Paul stopped and looked back at her.

"I was going to stretch my legs."

The bag in his hand, he continued staring at her as she held open the door of the car.

"You don't want me to stretch my legs." She moved her foot back into the car.

"I'm sorry I don't have the authority to let you roam the grounds."

"Well do you think it would be all right if I were to walk down and try to find a place to eat."

"You didn't eat anything when you got up."

"I didn't feel you'd want me to eat your food."

"And you didn't think to ask."

"I said I wasn't going to bother you."

Paul glanced up at the house, then back at Laura. Reaching into his pocket, he walked to the car. "You may as well take the car and find a place to eat." He held out the keys to her.

"I might scratch it." She pulled the door closed. "I'll wait."

He returned the keys to his pocket. "You look awful, you know."

"I'm sure I do."

"I suppose you didn't do anything to your face before we left because you didn't think you should ask to use the bathroom."

"I didn't feel I should, no."

"Because I'd let you come in with me if you didn't look so awful." He looked at the rearview mirror. "Can you fix yourself up a little in that?"

"You don't have to let me come in."

"But I don't want you sitting out here either."

She moved to the center of the seat and opened her purse.

"I suppose you need to go to the bathroom too."

She brought up a small hairbrush and began brushing her hair.

"Well do you?"

"I can wait."

"I guess you thought it would put me out to ask to stop at a gas station on the way up."

"You were preoccupied." She pulled the brush down through her hair.

"Now I see why you wanted to walk around the grounds so badly." He pulled open the car door. "Come in with me."

"I haven't put on my lipstick."

"There isn't time."

Laura stepped out of the car.

"And don't say anything in here. Is that understood?"

"Yes, Paul."

They walked across fallen eucalyptus leaves, then climbed one of the two stairways leading up to a stone terrace and a small portico over the front door. Paul pressed a brass button beside the heavy wooden door, then stood moving his bag from one hand to the other as he waited. Laura fixed her eyes on the lower part of the door, till finally it was pulled slowly open.

Inside sat a thin, small man in a wheelchair. "Paul Grove?" he said, frowning up at Paul.

"Yes, sir. You're Mr. Davis."

The man wheeled himself backward and they stepped inside.

"Close the door."

Laura took a large handle on the inside of the door and pushed it closed.

"They said you'd be alone," the man said.

"I needed some help."

The man wheeled forward to the door and fixed a chain in place. "I asked if there'd be more than one and they said there wouldn't." He turned to Laura. "What's your name then."

"Miss Haine," Paul said. "She won't be in the way."

"My wife's dead seventeen years, Miss Haine."

"We'll try not to be long," Paul said, starting toward a flight of stairs.

"Where's your equipment."

"The big equipment won't be coming until next month," he said. "You'll be told about all that by Mr. Gar."

"I didn't like Mr. Gar."

Paul motioned for Laura.

"You tell Mr. Gar I don't want more than eight people on the property at once."

Paul started up the wide wooden staircase and Laura followed.

"Did you hear what I said?"

"I'll tell him."

"Miss Haine," he called, "I outlived my house servant twelve years next August."

She glanced back at him, sitting at the foot of the stairs in his chair.

"What do you think of that."

"Yes, I heard you."

"I'll bury them all." He pointed up at her with a narrow finger. "I'll bury you." He laughed, turned in his chair and wheeled himself out of sight into another room.

They walked up past a landing to the second story. Inside an open door ahead of them was the end of a low bathtub.

"If you have to go to the bathroom," Paul said, "go now."

"Thank you." She walked through the door and closed it behind her. After setting her purse on the floor of large black and white tiles, she stepped to a framed photograph on the wall showing a young man in a white undershirt, a broad stripe slanting across it as he stood astride his bicycle to accept a tall silver trophy. She bent closer and squinted slightly to study the features of the man downstairs.

Paul was up on the third story when she came out. She heard a click, walked to the base of the stairway and could see him at the top, seated and aiming his camera down. "Move," he said.

She stepped over to the side of the stair.

"Get out of the picture."

"Come up?"

"Up or down. But move."

She hurried on up the stairs as he pressed the lever on the top of the camera.

"I didn't know what you meant."

He went to a wall and looked at the baseboard running along the bottom of it, aimed the camera and clicked it again. Winding it, he pushed open the door of a bedroom, raised the camera again and took a picture of a large fourposter bed. Then he turned toward a marble-topped bureau with a round mirror rising up from it in a carved wooden frame. He fell to one knee, brought up his camera and photographed it. Walking forward on his knees he took another, then got down on his elbows and took a picture of one of its brass feet, winding the camera when he was through.

"I guess it wouldn't be my business to ask why you're doing this."

He walked around on his knees to the other side of the bureau.

"My husband does technical writing for magazines," she said. "I just wondered if you might work for a magazine too."

"Pull that curtain away from the sash."

Laura went to the window and took hold of the bottom of a heavy lace curtain.

"Hold it away."

She pulled it toward her.

"You're in the picture."

She stepped back.

"Get your leg out."

Holding the end of the curtain, she stepped as far as she could away from the window. Paul clicked the shutter. "I'll do the kitchen next so you can get something to eat." Winding the camera, he walked back past her and into the hall. He bent over to pick up his bag from beside a post supporting the banister and started down.

"I'd want to ask the man before I took something to eat."

"Don't ask him anything."

There was a squeaking noise as they neared the bottom, and the wheelchair appeared below. "Coming down?" the man said.

"I'd like a minute or two in your kitchen. I'll need the measurements in there so when the others come they'll know what space they have to work in."

The man looked at Laura. "He wants to measure my kitchen."

"If you could just tell me where it is," Paul said.

"Did I hear the plumbing?" the man said, frowning.

"I used the bathroom," Laura said.

"Don't use things if you don't ask. You're not here to use things."

"The kitchen," Paul said.

The man pointed toward a doorway and they started toward it.

"You want to use the toilet again, you tell me first. That's not the one we use." He wheeled away.

In the kitchen Paul removed a measuring tape from his bag and stretched it across an enamel-covered table. Then he let it snap back into its case and pulled open the door of the refrigerator. "Have something to eat."

"No."

Paul set down the tape measure and pulled out a carton of milk. He carried it to a cupboard, opened the door and took down a heavy rose-tinged glass. He filled it and returned the milk carton to the refrigerator.

"I hope that's not for me."

He held out the glass.

"Really," she said.

"You're my guest here, not his."

"But I'm not going to drink it without telling him."

Paul poured the milk out into the sink and set the empty glass on the shelf, then picked up his tape measure again.

Laura walked to the sink.

"What are you doing."

"I'm going to wash the glass."

"No you're not."

"Paul," she said, "I don't know what your business is here or who this man is or what all this is about. But it's unnecessary to go to this much trouble to hurt someone's feelings, and I'm not going to let you." She picked up the glass and turned on the faucet.

It was an hour later, after he'd finished inside and they were on the grounds, that Laura spoke to him again. He'd just taken a photograph of the roof of the house from the rear of the property and was copying figures into his notebook.

Laura sat on the cracked rim of a small concrete pool, the broken statue of a child playing a mouth instrument rising out of the center of it from a bed of eucalyptus pods. She twirled a leaf by its stem and let it fall.

"Would you mind taking a walk?" Paul said, reaching into his bag for a lens. He read something on the side of it, then returned it.

"You don't enjoy your work very much, do you."

"What I don't enjoy is being harassed *while* I work."

She watched him start on the next page. "It's past noon, you know."

"I don't get hungry at the stroke of twelve." He glanced at a path running between several brown bushes on the other side of the pool. "Why don't you explore through there."

"There's something I want to ask you."

"When you come back you can ask."

She got up, went past the broken figure in the pool and down the path. Beyond the bushes it turned and stopped abruptly at a high wire fence. She looked through the rusted wire at a long brown lawn, some trees at the far end of it, then turned around and went back the way she had come.

Paul had seated himself and was leaning against a tree, erasing something in the notebook. "That wasn't a walk."

"There was a fence in the way."

"Go in another direction."

"You said after I walked, I could ask, and now I'm going to ask you something about what you said last night."

Paul brushed the bits of eraser from his pad. "Was the den off the living room or off the hall."

"You told me I felt superior to you. And it was against your principles to help me for that reason."

"Or was it off the dining room," he said. "Yes, it was off the dining room." He began writing again.

"Just tell me what I've done to make you think I feel superior to you."

"Don't talk about this," he said as his pencil moved ahead. "I don't want to argue today."

"You know, sometimes you act so much like John I could close my eyes and believe I was talking to him. And I do know why you don't want to talk about this. Because you *like* to tell yourself people feel superior to you, so you won't have to admit it's the other way around."

The pencil stopped.

"And it makes me mad to be told I feel superior to someone when I don't. And it makes me madder that once you say it you refuse to discuss it. Because that way you can go around thinking what a snob I am for looking down on homosexuals."

Paul cleared his throat softly. "I'll be through soon. I know you're hungry."

"God, you think you're so cool," she said, walking away from him. "I'll be in the car."

It was over an hour before Paul returned. He got in, backed the car out and drove down the driveway. The large gates swung open as they neared the bottom, and the car passed through. They wound down curving streets till reaching a highway. Paul drove over a small bridge that crossed it and then along a side road to where tall bushes grew up beside the gray peeling walls of a building. "This is a restaurant. I've eaten here before."

Laura got out and walked ahead of him to the building, but a blind was pulled down on the other side of the glass door. She turned the knob but it didn't open.

"Closed?" he called from behind her.

"Well, it's not open, is it."

Paul got into the car again, but Laura stayed where she was. He reached over to open the door. "If the place is closed, get back in the car."

She walked to a small table and a bench beside the restaurant. She seated herself and looked off in the other direction from the highway.

Paul shifted the engine into reverse and slowly backed the car next to the table. "I'm going to find a place to eat, are you coming?"

She kept her eyes turned toward a cliff that dropped off to the sea beyond the restaurant.

Paul sat looking at her for a few moments, then picked up her purse from the seat and held it out the door. "Here's this."

She didn't turn her head.

"Take it. I'm going."

"I've come to the conclusion," she said, "that I don't have to be treated this way by you anymore."

Paul leaned farther across the seat, then tossed the purse so it landed at the edge of the table. "Grab it. It's about to fall to the ground."

She caught it as it began to slide off the table.

"There's a bus station across the highway." He pulled the door closed. "I think one leaves every hour for Los Angeles."

"I don't want to be left."

"Then get in."

"I won't be treated this way anymore."

"What way."

"You know what way."

"Look, if anyone's treating anyone badly, you've got it backwards. You insult me while I try to work. You purposely get in my way. I mean I can be patient to a point. Your husband walked out on you, abandoned you. Okay, I get the picture. But don't keep pushing it so hard, Laura."

She looked down at the purse in her hand.

"I mean I don't know what you want."

"Yes you do."

"Do you want me to get out of the car?"

"That would be something."

He turned off the motor and slid across the seat. "I'll get out of the car," he said, getting out. "Okay, I'm out."

She glanced at him.

"So I'm out of the car. You told me you'd like me to get out of the car and I did."

"You don't realize that when you act the way you do toward someone else it's very painful for them."

"What else should I do."

"Would it be a violation of your code," she said, turning to him, "to tell me what you're doing here, why you were doing what you were at the man's house this morning?"

"Why do you need to know."

"But why shouldn't I."

Paul looked down at the crumpled paper cup in the gravel next to one of the legs of the bench on which she was seated.

"Why."

"It's my work."

"I know that, but what kind of work is it."

"Taking pictures and measuring."

"But for what reason? For who?"

He bent down and picked up the cup. "I'll try not to treat you badly. If you feel I am, tell me. I'll try to stop." He rested the cup on the table.

"You don't feel it's unfair not to tell me the kind of work you do."

"There's nothing about it that has to do with you," he said. "I apologize for saying I was going to leave you, but I'm hungry now, so if you'll get back in the car I want to find a place to eat."

She looked at the open door of the car. "Don't you think it's just a little thoughtless not to tell me where you're staying tonight or what I'm supposed to do, or anything like that?"

"I don't know where I'm staying."

"You don't have someone to stay with."

"No."

"Will you sleep in the car?"

"No."

"On the beach? I mean I don't know what to expect."

"I don't sleep on the beach."

"Well where then. A motel?"

"I suppose."

"But why didn't you just say that." She got up from the bench. "If you knew what I was asking you, why couldn't you just say you were sleeping in a motel." She climbed back into her side of the car. "You lead me through pointless guessing games, then act surprised when I wonder why you just didn't come out with the answer to my question when I asked it."

Paul walked around to the front of the car. "I usually find somewhere to stay before I start work," he said as he got in. "I didn't this time because you were with me."

"Well you should have."

"I guess I just feel strange about us being seen together."

She looked down at an ashtray built into the armrest on the door. "Paul, who would it make any difference to."

"You don't care if it's the same motel then."

She turned to him. "We're talking about a place to sleep. I don't think either of us is contemplating anything besides that. Are we?"

"I wasn't."

The motel they chose that night was the first one they came to after dinner, a mile farther down the highway from the restaurant, and the room was the last one in a long row of cabins. Paul carried his bag in and set it on one of the two small beds. "I put my things on that one," he said as Laura came in after him, "but I didn't mean for you to interpret it as meaning I had to sleep in it, if you prefer it."

She glanced at the bed, then turned back toward the door. "I think I'll go for a walk on the beach."

"Well what about the beds."

"It doesn't matter."

"Okay, just one thing before you go, if we could have it in mind ahead of time a little about how we're going to retire when the time comes."

"You mean how we're going to sleep?"

"Just generally. I guess we *could* sleep in our clothes."

"I'll sleep in my slip."

He nodded. "I see. Now as far as removing your dress goes, you'd do that . . . where would you do that."

"Why is this important to you."

"You don't want to tell me."

She glanced at the bathroom. "If you need a plan about it, then I'll do it in there."

"You'd go first then? Before I did?"

"Why don't you decide in what order we undress, Paul."

"I just want to get all this straight beforehand. There are conflicting questions in my mind."

"That we'll accidentally see each other as we take off our clothes?"

"Partly."

"We won't see each other's bodies, Paul."

"You're sure."

"Yes, Paul."

He looked at the chair beside Laura with two white antimacassars on its arms.

"If you'd like, you can go in the bathroom and get ready, and while you're in there I'll take off my dress and get in bed and that way you won't even have to see my slip."

"I just want it to go smoothly."

"It will, Paul." She stepped to the door and reached for the knob, but then stopped. Outside a car drove over the gravel and parked in front of the cabin beside theirs. "Paul, behind all this strange conversation we're having there isn't some thought coming from somewhere that you *want* to see me undress."

"It's not coming from me."

"Because if there's anything in your mind beyond just sleeping in here, then we will get two rooms and you'll loan me the money to pay for mine because I only have two dollars left."

"Why do you say I would have any thought beyond that."

"Because you keep going on and on about all this."

He looked down at the top of his suitcase. "If there was such a thought, you'd hate me, wouldn't you."

"Paul," she said, "I wouldn't hate you. But you do have other thoughts than just sleeping tonight, don't you."

He walked to a window and pushed back a small curtain. "I might."

"You do."

"You hate me."

"No. But I'll just have to get another room."

He watched a wave break on the sand. "You don't call that hating. Someone expresses affection for you and you get a different room."

"I call it realizing another person has feelings you didn't think he had."

"Of loving you."

She rested her hand on the lace doily on the back of the armchair. "Paul, I really don't think you love me."

"I guess I'm not capable of that, am I."

"You may be capable of it. But under the circumstances, I don't think you do."

"What about this then," he said. "What if I paid you to see your breasts?"

She looked down at her hand.

"What about that. You said you need extra money."

She shook her head.

"Why, because no amount of money would be enough to show them to anyone as disgusting as me?"

The door closed in the room beside theirs.

"Because I don't show my breasts to people for money, Paul."

"What about your husband," he said, turning around.

"He doesn't pay me to see my breasts."

"But he sees them."

"Yes, Paul."

He took a step toward her. "He thinks nothing of walking out on you, leaving you no one to turn to till I offer my help. I jeopardize my work to see that you don't have to be alone. And now I ask you a tiny favor, one you think nothing of doing for a man who mistreats you."

"Paul, we don't see the situation in the same perspective."

"You don't think I desire to know the beauty of your inner self."

"Paul."

"Isn't that true."

"No."

"Then why else won't you."

"We'd stand here till tomorrow if I tried to make you understand, so I'll just ask you if this is going to go on."

"If what is."

"Your request for me to undress in front of you. If it is, I'll get another room."

"What if you bring it up again yourself."

"I won't, Paul."

"Okay then." He walked to his bag on the bed. "I was just making sure you didn't have anything in your mind about something happening between us. You've satisfied me that you don't."

HERE had been a second phonecall over the weekend to Laura's parents from the man who had called before. Laura's father had copied down a name and an address on a small piece of paper beside their phone. He gave it to her when she came for the children.

At twenty minutes before ten on Monday morning, holding the piece of paper in her hand, Laura left her car in the parking lot of an office building several blocks from her house. She walked into the lobby and to the directory of occupants. Beside the list of firms was an elevator standing open. She got onto it and took it to the twelfth floor. Then she walked down a hall till she saw a door with the names DECKER, CONWAY & WASHINGTON on it and pushed it open.

A girl seated behind a small switchboard looked up.

"I have an appointment with Mr. Washington," Laura said as the door closed behind her.

"I don't believe Mr. Washington's come in yet, but I'll tell his secretary you're here." She pushed one of her cords into the switchboard. "There's a woman here for Mr. Washington." She listened a moment, then removed the cord. "She'll be right out. Will you be seated?"

Laura glanced at the chair against the wall. "I had a call from him to come at ten."

"I'm sure he'll be here then. Excuse me." She pushed another cord into the board. "Decker, Conway and Washington. Good morning." Laura walked to the chair and sat down. "One moment, please, I'll connect you." The girl removed the cord and inserted it into another hole.

"I had another question too," Laura said.

"One minute please, I want to make sure they pick up." She listened into her earphone, then looked back at Laura.

"I was gone for the weekend. Yesterday afternoon I went to pick up my children at my parents' house and my father had the message from Mr. Washington. He'd called a first time and hadn't said who it was, then called again and asked for the appointment, but he didn't leave any details, and I wondered if. . . ."

"Excuse me." The girl pulled out another cord. "Decker, Conway and Washington. Good morning." She listened a moment. "I'm sorry, Mr. Ashford is no longer with the firm." She smiled. "Thank you. Goodbye." She looked back at Laura. "Were you the lady who left two messages on the answering recorder last night?"

"I was."

"Because I thought I'd recognized your voice when you came in, but I wasn't positive."

"I want to find out what Mr. Washington needs to see me about."

"Oh, here's Peggy."

A red-haired girl had stepped into the room from

the other direction. She bent forward slightly toward Laura. "Mrs. Foster? Will you come with me?"

Laura got up and followed her along a hallway past a woman typing, then around a corner to a desk beside which was a door with Mr. Washington's name printed on it in neat gold letters. "You're a little early," the girl said as she seated herself on a chair behind the desk. "Mr. Washington always comes in just at ten." She held her hand out toward the chair across from hers.

"Thank you," Laura said as she sat. "I was asking the receptionist what the appointment was for."

The girl looked down at an open appointment book in front of her. "It's at ten."

"I know," Laura said. "I just didn't know *what* it was for. *You* don't know why he wants to see me."

"I wish I did Mrs. Foster, but it's just eight minutes till ten. He's never late."

"Can you tell me what kind of a lawyer he is?"

The girl pushed the appointment book to the side of the desk. "It's hard to say just what kind. I know he's very busy with a case where the city is trying to collect from a contractor for a bridge that's cracking, if that's any help."

There was a round clock on the wall behind the secretary and as the large hand moved to the number at the top a man in a gray suit stepped around the corner of the hall. "Good morning, Peggy," he said as he walked past her and opened the door with his name on it.

"Good morning, Mr. Washington. Mrs. Foster is here."

He walked through the door and closed it behind him.

"He'll see you in a moment," she said, "he likes to look at his mail first. He won't read it till later, but he likes to see what it is before his first appointment."

Laura nodded.

"I always have his tea ready for him, but the boy hasn't come by yet."

They sat quietly for a few moments, then there was a buzz from a small box on the desk between them. "He'll see you now."

Laura got up and walked to the door. Pushing it open, she could see Mr. Washington seated behind his large desk. "Come in, Mrs. Foster. I'm Clarence Washington." He picked up a small stack of mail, tapped on its end to neaten it, then put it in a drawer in front of him and pushed it closed. "Please be seated."

She walked to a leather-covered chair on her side of the desk and eased herself down onto it.

Mr. Washington reached out to press a button on his desk. A moment later the secretary looked into the room. "Peggy, I don't see my tea."

"The boy didn't come this morning, Mr. Washington, would you like me to call down and see where he is?"

"If you could."

She stepped back and closed the door.

Mr. Washington cleared his throat softly. He sat a moment with his eyes cast down toward his blotter, then turned slightly in his swivel chair and looked across the desk at Laura. "Quite a nip for this time of year," he said.

She moved forward on her chair. "Mr. Washington,

I phoned twice last night to learn what the appointment's for."

"I haven't played my telephone tapes yet."

"I would just like to know what it is you want."

Mr. Washington smiled. "This tea of mine is something I've grown accustomed to over the years. Usually Peggy has it here, though they've got a new boy downstairs and I'm not sure he's working out. Would you like anything, Mrs. Foster?"

"No."

"Let's see what Peggy's found out." He pressed the button on his desk again.

In a moment the door opened and Peggy looked through. "Mr. Washington, the boy didn't come down to this end of the hall, but they're sending him right up."

"Thank you."

The door closed.

"Mr. Washington."

"You'll have to forgive my little quirk with the tea," he said. "I really don't feel like I'm quite here till I've had the first sip. I hope you weren't waiting long."

"Sir," she said, "could I just ask you one thing. Is this something about John?"

His head moved forward an inch and he raised his eyebrows.

"John. My husband. Is it about my husband."

He sat back in the chair again. "The tea is coming, Mrs. Foster. Let's just try to take one thing at a time."

"Last Friday afternoon my husband and I were planning to leave for a weekend trip to Lake Tahoe. I left the children at my parents' house. When I got back John was gone. He hasn't been back since. So could you please tell me if this has to do with him?"

Mr. Washington placed the ends of his fingers together before him.

"He may be hurt," Laura said.

"Let's put it this way," Mr. Washington said, looking up at her over his fingers. "Although I can't tell you whether it's to do with your husband or not, I can say that if it should be to do with him, I wouldn't be the one to bring you news of an accident."

"Then he's all right."

"Mrs. Foster, I'm simply trying to make it clear to you that if something happened to your husband you would not have been notified by a lawyer."

"But you won't tell me if it's about him."

"Not till my tea comes."

Laura looked at him a moment, then glanced at the door. "Could I go down myself and bring up the tea?"

"Don't be silly."

Laura sat back in her chair.

When the tea came it was in a white styrofoam cup with the end of the string from the tea bag hanging over its edge. In her other hand, Peggy carried a napkin with a thin slice of lemon resting in the center of it. She walked to Mr. Washington's desk and set them down on the blotter. "The little plate," he said. "The little paper plate."

"He didn't bring one."

"Well this is what happens." He pointed at a dark-ish circle on his blotter.

"Yes, sir."

"Call office supplies and tell them if they don't want to replace my blotter on a daily basis they'd better look into this."

"Yes, Mr. Washington." She backed toward the door.

"And while you're at it, Peggy, call Food Services too. Tell them the tea was cold yesterday, there was no plate two days ago and no plate today. And tell them that you already told them there was no plate two days ago but there still was no plate today. And tell them it was ten minutes late."

"I told them that."

"And tell them I don't see why they keep this new boy on."

"Yes, sir." She stepped through the door and closed it.

He lifted the tea bag up by its string and dunked it several times in the water. "For the rent they get I think I'm owed a few amenities from the management."

Laura watched as he dipped the bag in the cup several times more. Then he rested the sopping bag on the napkin, picked up the lemon and squeezed it into his tea. "I have no napkin now," he said. "I've had to use the napkin for the bag, because there was no plate, so now I have no napkin."

"Do you want a Kleenex?"

Mr. Washington shook his head. He gathered the tea bag and lemon peel up in the napkin and dropped them into a wastebasket under his desk. Then he took a swallow of the tea, returned the cup to his blotter and sat back in his chair. "Let's get started here," he said. "Mrs. Foster, you were mentioning your weekend to me. Let's start there. Tell me. How was your weekend. Did you have a good weekend."

Laura looked down at the styrofoam cup on the desk.

"You've told me you left your children at your parents' house on Friday, I assume it was Friday, and came back to find your husband gone after the two of you had planned a trip."

"Yes."

"Did you go to Lake Tahoe alone?"

"No."

"Did you stay in your house all weekend? I know you didn't do that because I phoned there. Did you stay with friends? What did you do."

She looked up at his face.

"You don't have to tell me. I simply thought it would be useful for us to talk in a casual manner until we felt more comfortable with each other."

"You said when your tea came you'd tell me why I'm here."

"And I will." He reached for the tea and moved it to his lap.

"You called my house," she said. "Then you called my father. The first time you talked to him you didn't, or wouldn't, I don't know which, say who it was. I was distressed when I got that message."

"You got that message."

"Yes, my father told me you called."

"When."

She looked at the blotter where a dark circle had been left by the bottom of the cup. "Well I guess he told me Friday night."

"You saw him Friday night."

"I didn't see him Friday night, but I talked to him by phone and he said you'd called."

"May I ask where you called him from."

"Lake Tahoe," she said, looking up.

"I thought you didn't go to Lake Tahoe."

"I didn't get all the way up."

"How far up did you get."

"Mr. Washington."

"You went home Friday afternoon," he said, reaching for a pad of paper at the side of the desk and removing a black pen from its holder. "You found your husband gone. You got in the car and drove partway up to Lake Tahoe in time to call your father that night. Do you remember the name of the hotel or motel where you registered Friday night?"

For several moments Laura continued to look at him. "Mr. Washington," she said finally, "where I stayed, or what I did, over the weekend has nothing to do with anything. What I came here to talk about is the purpose of your two phonecalls to my father, the first one where you wouldn't identify yourself, and the second where you wouldn't tell him what you wanted. You've had your tea. Now what do you want."

Slowly, Mr. Washington lowered his pen and rested it diagonally on the sheet of memo paper in front of him. "I guess we have to get around to that sooner or later, don't we."

"Yes, Mr. Washington."

"I'd thought perhaps we could take our time, but that doesn't seem to be the way you choose." He picked up his cup again, took a drink of the tea and placed it back on the blotter. "Mrs. Foster," he said, "your husband is my client."

She frowned slightly at him over the desk.

"My relationship to your husband is that I am his attorney and he is my client."

"Oh."

"Does that clear up any of the mystery."

"Well, why does he need an attorney."

"That's the next step, Mrs. Foster, but first let's make sure we understand the relationship between the three of us. You are his wife, and I am his lawyer. I am his representative. Do we understand that."

"I don't know why he needs a representative."

"I appreciate that, but you do understand that's what I am."

She shrugged. "If you say so."

"You understand that I am representing him to you."

"You keep saying it. Of course I understand. It's just that there's no reason. There isn't . . . any. . . ." Very gradually, her eyes fixed on the cup of tea, Laura's shoulders slumped downward. "It doesn't . . . I mean there's only one reason, right off hand, that I could think of. I know it isn't the one. But the only reason I could think of for him having a lawyer . . . call me in . . . represent him to me. . . ." Her brow slowly knitted into two deep furrows. "But there's no reason for that. And he'd talk about it with me. We *have* talked about it."

"What's that, Mrs. Foster."

"He'd discuss it with me. It wouldn't be like this. He'd never have it like this." She watched as Mr. Washington pulled open the drawer at the side of his desk. "If anyone's wrong, it's John, it's not me." He removed a folded form from the desk and closed the drawer. "Because we've talked about it, but he knows that's not the answer." She looked down as Mr. Washington placed the folded piece of paper on the desk between them. "Listen. You know, the last time this subject came up, a few months ago, we talked about counseling. We're going to try counseling. Mr. Washington, I have the name of a counselor from a good friend, Grace Crawford. They live right in back of us. I don't have the name with me, but we're going to see him. He shouldn't have called you about this. He should have waited." Her eyes fell to the form on the desk in front of her and she studied the black wording.

"It's a legal formality that I hand this document to you, Mrs. Foster," he said, "so if you're finished, I'll hand it to you, and that part we can have behind us."

"I won't take it."

"It's called serving it to you, Mrs. Foster. In legal terms, you're called the defendant. Your husband is the plaintiff. One of the responsibilities of the plaintiff's attorney is to physically hand the summons, which we call this piece of paper, to the defendant, thereby technically discharging the duty of informing the defendant of the intent of the plaintiff to sue. This is the purpose of your coming here."

"Sue."

"If you don't take it," he said, "it will still constitute the serving of the summons on you by my having offered it to you and explaining its purpose. So it doesn't help either of us for you not to take it."

"I won't take it," she said, looking up at him. "I respect that John has asked you to do this. I know you think he wants you to. I'm not blaming you for getting involved in this, but after I've talked to him we can pay you your fee for taking up your time, if you're worried about that, and go our different ways." She got up from the chair.

"Mrs. Foster."

"No," she said. "You don't know John. You don't know him. I'll straighten this out with him and get in touch with you again. You send the bill." She walked toward the door.

"Where is he now, Mrs. Foster?"

She stopped.

"If you're going to straighten things out with him, you'll need to talk to him." Mr. Washington got up from his chair.

"I'll find him," she said, turning around to face him.

He gestured toward the leather easy chair. "We must discuss this intelligently, Mrs. Foster. For your sake, for John's and for the sake of your children."

"Don't worry about my children, Mr. Washington."

"I am worried about them."

"This is a matter between John and me," she said, taking a step toward him. "I will straighten it out, and you will be sent a check."

"Do stop talking about money, Mrs. Foster. My fee arrangements have been worked out between your husband and myself."

"Then I'll send you a check for this visit."

He pulled the chair partway around to face her.

"Do you know where he is?" she said.

"Yes."

"Will you tell me?"

"I'm not free to tell you." He rested his hand on the back of the chair.

"Somewhere there's a law, Mr. Washington, that says you have to tell the wife where the husband is, if she wants to know."

"Under these circumstances, Mrs. Foster, that is not correct."

"Even though it would lead to my discussing things with him in a way that would avoid what's happening, you still won't tell me."

"My client doesn't believe further talk would help."

"Well it would help," she said, "and I'll tell you something else. I can find John."

"Through his partner, Mr. Pardee?"

"That's one way."

"I spoke to Mr. Pardee over the weekend, Mrs. Foster, to inform him that I alone have been entrusted with his whereabouts, and that if any communications are necessary between Mr. Foster and Mr. Pardee, other than those initiated by your husband, they are to go through me."

"So I shouldn't try to get it out of Roger."

"To be blunt, no."

Laura shook her head. "Then I'll find another way."

"Your husband needs privacy very badly right now, Mrs. Foster."

"May I ask you how long you've known John."

"That's immaterial, Mrs. Foster. It's necessary only that I've spent enough time with him to know his wishes as they affect the duties I am to perform for him."

Laura returned to the chair. "If you knew, really, what there was between John and me. I mean you think. . . ." She seated herself. "This is so frustrating, because you don't know John *or* me."

Mr. Washington walked around to his side of the desk.

"He's not going to do it, Mr. Washington." She watched him sit down. "You got some instructions about some duties he asked you to perform. But for him to have a stranger call me up and ask me into his office to tell me he's divorcing me just isn't something John is capable of being serious about. It isn't."

Mr. Washington opened a folder on the desk in front of himself. "The first thing I should advise you to do is find an attorney."

"Oh no."

"Perhaps your family has a lawyer you could speak to."

She placed her hand on the printed form between them. "May I just look at this for a moment?"

"It's yours."

"I don't need to keep it," she said, picking it up and

opening it. "I was just curious about the grounds he chose." She looked at it a few moments, then returned it to the blotter. "Really. He's a subtle person. If he were serious about this, the last thing he'd do would be to pick something as obvious as mental cruelty. That's just a cliché."

"There are only a limited number of grounds for divorce, Mrs. Foster."

"Mr. Washington, the thing you don't know about John, and I don't say this unkindly, it's just one of his attitudes, and I don't love him any less for it, maybe even more, but he lives in a world where he feels persecuted by those around him. He's always felt that way. As a child. Always. And I tell him that if anyone ever took that feeling away from him he'd be lost. And it's true. And you wouldn't know that, because you don't know him. And you don't know that every time he loses a sale of an article he's written . . . he's a writer, you know."

"I know, Mrs. Foster."

"Well every time he doesn't get something bought by a magazine it's my fault. Or the children's. Or even the neighbors'. But it's never John's fault. We used to have a dog and it was even the dog's fault when one of his articles wasn't bought by the magazine. Now we just have a gold-fish. So I guess when he doesn't make a sale now it's Henry the goldfish's fault." She looked past Mr. Washington and out the window at a building in the distance.

"Mrs. Foster."

"I agree that it's alarming that he's gone this far this time. It's probably because of the problems in his writing that he hasn't mentioned to me. He's joined up with Roger in partnership. They're both writers, they got an office together about two months ago. Probably there are difficulties there he hasn't told me. But you shouldn't get caught up in these theories of his about how it's everyone else's fault because when it's all over he'll apologize for taking up everyone's time and we'll all feel foolish."

Mr. Washington reached for the divorce paper and moved it toward himself.

"You don't believe me, but it's true."

"Let's both suspend our judgments for the time being," he said.

"In the end we can suspend judgment all we want but the last laugh will be on us. I've been through this."

"You don't want to suspend judgment."

"I know him too well."

He opened the form in front of him. His eyes remained on it for several moments. "I'm going to bring up the subject of you finding an attorney a final time," he said. "What I have to say next would be much better brought up with a lawyer of yours than by me."

"I agree."

He looked up.

"If it were serious," she said, "that would be how to do it. But it isn't."

He looked back at the page. "Mrs. Foster," he said, "there is an unusual feature of this divorce suit. Personally, I haven't taken a case before in which such a feature was included. And because it's bound to cause emotion, I feel reluctant to get into it without your having an attorney."

"What's the unusual feature."

He leaned back in his chair. "Let me ask you something, Mrs. Foster. You had a psychiatrist till recently, didn't you."

"I'm sure John told you I did."

"Yes," he said, "but I wonder if you could tell me what originally brought you and your husband to decide on your need for one."

She looked down at the desk.

"If you could do that, very briefly."

"I'd be glad to do it. I don't know what point there is in it. It was a lot of things."

Mr. Washington nodded.

"It wasn't just one thing."

"I understand."

"The strongest reason I went to him was to ease the pressure on John."

Mr. Washington frowned.

"He wanted me to go and I went."

"He asked you to go, you could see it would ease his pressure, so you agreed."

"Yes."

"That was very thoughtful of you. Did you go a long time? How long did you go."

Laura bit her lip as she studied the top of the desk. "It's hard to remember, exactly."

"Approximately."

"About two years." She looked up. "Maybe a few weeks one way or the other."

Mr. Washington kept his eyes on the desk. "I had the opportunity to speak to Dr. Munger over the weekend."

"It might not have been quite that long," she said.

"We talked to another one, but I didn't go to him." She cleared her throat. "Let's see. I think from the time the subject first came up till when I finished was about two years, that's what I was thinking. The time with Dr. Munger was less."

"Eleven months?"

She nodded. "That sounds right."

"Eleven months is more than a few weeks less than two years."

"I was thinking of the overall time we discussed it."

"Mrs. Foster," he said, running his finger slowly down the edge of the divorce paper, "maybe you could tell me the reasons for your leaving Dr. Munger. About eight months ago, as I understand it."

"About that."

"And you left for what reason."

"A number of reasons."

"But what stands out as being of especial importance."

She shrugged and looked up at him. "I guess John felt more relaxed and it didn't seem necessary to go anymore."

"John improved."

"It had helped him. There was no reason to keep pouring the money into it."

"In other words, then, you went to the doctor to relieve pressure on your husband, and when you felt the pressures were less you left him, because the purpose of helping your husband had been served."

"I'm sure John didn't see it that way."

"What happened when you left him. Did your husband thank you for seeing him while he was under the stress?"

"No."

"What did he do."

"I'm sure he's already gone into all this with you," she said. "He told me to go back."

"And what did you say."

"I said I'd gone enough."

"And what did he say."

"I guess he just kept telling me to go back."

"Was that all?"

"I guess we fought about it, if that's what you want to hear."

"I want to hear the truth, Mrs. Foster. Did he tell you he couldn't live with you unless you returned to Dr. Munger?"

"He may have."

"Did he, Mrs. Foster?"

"I'm sure he did."

"Do you remember him saying it?"

"Yes."

"But you declined to return."

"Why should I have gone back? I wasn't even the one who needed the psychiatrist in the first place."

"Mrs. Foster," he said, resting both hands on the piece of paper, "you've told me you went to Dr. Munger to ease the strain on your husband."

"Yes."

"Now you're telling me he wished you to continue.

Obviously, he felt strain again. He even made the condition that he couldn't live with you unless you returned. But you refused. I can't reconcile your two positions."

"It was different the second time."

"How was that."

"Who knows," she said. "I couldn't really say. It just seemed different."

Mr. Washington nodded.

"He'd gotten used to me going, and just wanted me to keep going."

"He took a personal pleasure in your going to see a psychiatrist."

"It seemed like it."

"It wasn't because he felt relieved to think you were getting treatment and help."

She shook her head. "Maybe he liked to think of me as mentally unbalanced."

"He liked to think of you as a little crazy."

"I don't know why else he would insist on it."

"When you left Dr. Munger, how did you work it out with the doctor. What agreement did the two of you come to at the end of your term."

"We didn't come to one."

"How did the separation occur then."

"I left."

"You made the decision."

"Yes."

"Did Dr. Munger do anything about it?"

"He tried to make me come back. He called me a few times."

"How many."

"Three or four," she said. "John had him call."

Mr. Washington pushed back his chair from the desk and stood. "Mrs. Foster, I had thought the way to get into the difficult feature of the suit would be through discussing your doctor with you. I can see that isn't going to work. So I'll say now, a last time, that if you don't go out of this office and hire yourself a lawyer, you are, in my opinion, a very naïve woman."

"I guess I'm naïve then."

"Yes. You are, Mrs. Foster. Because you'll certainly be hurt much more than you need to this way." He turned and walked to his window. He stood looking out through the glass several moments, then cleared his throat. "There are two occurrences which form the basis of your husband's action." He placed his hands together behind him. "Both Dr. Munger and your husband felt the first incident gave evidence that you needed immediate therapy. It was after that your husband insisted you go. And both felt the second incident, which occurred after you'd taken it upon yourself to interrupt your treatment, was clearly reason enough to require you to return. And your husband's statement that he could no longer live with you if you didn't go back was based on his belief that the second occurrence, which happened recently, I understand, showed you to be an unfit person. So you know which two incidents I'm referring to."

"I do."

"But you don't feel they were important enough to tell me as reasons for going to Dr. Munger."

"No."

He turned around and walked back to his desk. "Let's conclude here, Mrs. Foster," he said, sitting down. "I'll explain briefly what's going to happen."

"Mr. Washington, they weren't that important."

"That's not for me to decide."

"They've been blown out of proportion by John," she said, "and by the doctor, who has a very expensive office to maintain on La Cienega by keeping it filled with patients. But they weren't that important, and there were witnesses to each one."

"Yes," he said, "and at the appropriate time they'll be called to make their statements. But in the meantime, Mrs. Foster, let me state to you that in the divorce settlement your husband is asking custody of both your children."

Laura began to cough, raising one of her hands to cover her mouth, but still coughing, finally bringing both of her hands up over the lower part of her face, still not stopping.

"Are you all right, Mrs. Foster."

She wiped her eye with the back of her hand.

"You see, this all should have been done through the proper formalities."

"I'm all right," she said quietly, coughing just once more.

"I'll have Peggy bring you something."

She shook her head.

"These points won't be decided here, Mrs. Foster. A courtroom is the place to go into all this."

"They know it was an accident what happened to Tommy. The people who saw it know." She reached for the phone. "I want you to know he's wrong. I'm going to call one of the people who was there."

"The argument," he said, placing his own hand over the receiver, "isn't between you and me, but between you and your husband. And it's a judge who will make the decision."

"They know I'm not negligent, Mr. Washington, and that's what they'll say in court. But instead of all this drama over nothing, it might be better if you knew why it was that my husband didn't come home Friday. May I just see where it's written down about custody of the children?"

"Certainly." He opened the paper, ran his eyes down it, then turned it around and put the end of his forefinger at the beginning of a sentence.

"Custody of both minor children, Thomas John Foster, and Flora Foster, visitation privileges for the Plaintiff to be determined by the Court." She looked up at him. "Mr. Washington," she said. She shook her head and sat back in the chair. "I'm sorry, but I have to laugh."

"You may laugh here."

"I have to, Mr. Washington. Visitation privileges to be arranged by the court. Is that what it said?"

"Arranged. Determined."

"I wonder how Flora will enjoy me visiting her and John at the Blue Stallion Baths." She looked up. "Mr. Washington, I'm the children's mother. I don't have to discuss this nonsense with you. I'm their mother and they're my children and I've never done anything I shouldn't have."

He nodded.

"But I want to tell you something about your client that he may have left out."

"I'd like to hear it."

"Your client, Mr. Washington, has a problem. One which I don't think he'd want me to discuss. And out of delicacy I didn't. But if he wants to go to extremes about all this, you may as well know that in the last few months he's been playing at being a homosexual. Maybe you know of a court that would give the children to him under those circumstances, but I don't. The reason he didn't come back Friday wasn't because he wanted privacy, Mr. Washington, it was because he was with some men, and I can tell you their names, if you don't believe me, and I can tell you where they were, at least part of the time."

"I know their names." He leaned back slightly and pulled open the drawer of his desk. "Your husband didn't know the full name of one. Ellison, something like that."

"Elsinor."

He lifted up a small sheet of paper. "Yes." He returned it to his desk.

"May I see the piece of paper?"

"No." He pushed the drawer closed.

"It was Lee somebody. That was the other one."

"Mrs. Foster."

"That's the first name of the other person, isn't it."

"Your husband's contention for the grounds of this divorce is that your continual insults to his masculinity created within him a sexual crisis. His experiences with homosexuals, he informs me, never involved more than conversation. I can't be certain of the truth of that, but I wouldn't have taken the case if I didn't incline very strongly to a belief in his honesty on the subject. His need for involvement with homosexuals, as he explained it, was a result of the damage done to his sexual confidence by you. Damage which he feels can be stopped only by the act of divorce. Damage, Mrs. Foster, which will, he is convinced, and I've spoken with Dr. Munger on this point, and he's not unsympathetic to it, drive your husband into practicing homosexuality, whereas up till now it's only been a testing of himself to try and learn if the fearfulness he's experiencing over his sexuality is because of you, or for other reasons." He held the form across the desk to her.

"And my children?"

"He feels your attitude toward men is a threat to the healthy development of your son."

"And Flora?"

"He doesn't want them to be separated."

She glanced at the paper, then took it.

"Your husband spent last night in the garage of your home because he feared to leave you alone in the house with the children. An arrangement with Grace Crawford, the neighbor you mentioned, has been worked out whereby she'll spend the next few nights in your home so your husband's mind will be at ease about the children's safety." Mr. Washington got up and walked to the door of his office. He turned the knob and pulled it open. "Peggy will see you out."

$\mathcal{W}$HEN Grace Crawford came she walked into the driveway and pushed open the door at the side of Laura's house. Then she carried a small overnight bag in onto the back porch. "Are you home?" she said, letting the door close after her. She started slightly to see Laura in the next room, sitting at the kitchen table. "I didn't see you there." She looked at her a moment, then stepped inside. "The car wasn't in the driveway and I didn't know if you were here." She walked into the kitchen. "You usually have the car outside. I always notice it on my way to the store." She put the small bag down on the linoleum floor. "Isn't the car usually out during the day? I thought I usually saw it there." She looked at the kitchen windows, then back at Laura. "Let's see now."

Laura got up from her chair. "Come upstairs, Grace. I'll show you your room."

"May I say something first, Laura?"

Laura walked to the traveling bag and picked it up. "We both know why you're here. There's no reason to apologize."

"I just want to tell you how silly I think this all is, Laura."

"Do you want to see your room?"

"I want you to believe me."

"I don't believe you, Grace." She turned and carried the bag out of the room.

"Frank asked me to come, Laura. I told him I thought it was ridiculous. Totally ridiculous." She followed Laura through the dining room. "He said he'd promised John that I would, and I just didn't want to take the time to argue about it." They started up the stairs. "Anyway, Laura, it's a chance for us to see each other, that's the way I look at it. We haven't really talked for weeks. And we can make it fun if we try. I know we can." At the top of the stairs Grace stopped beside a closed door. From the other side came the sound of a television.

"The children," Laura said.

"They don't get home till three." Grace turned to look at her.

"They were let out early, Grace," she said, continuing down the hall. "In a moment you can go in and see if I harmed them before you got here. Your room's at the end."

Grace hurried after her into the room. "Laura, listen."

Laura set the bag down and turned around to face her. "You're a hypocrite, Grace," she said, "and I didn't know that before. You're a hypocrite to be here, and you're a worse hypocrite to try and pretend everything's fine."

"Between you and me it is, Laura."

"No, Grace."

"I just know Frank wants me here, Laura. That's all I know."

"You believe I'm a threat to my children."

"Oh no, Laura."

"And it seems to me that to let you spend the night here in my house would give me the right to ask you to be honest with me."

Grace looked at her bag on the end of the bed.

"It seems to me the minimum I could ask is that you don't lie to me, Grace."

Grace seated herself beside the carrying case.

"You think I'm a menace to my children, or you wouldn't be here."

"Please don't say that."

"I do say it."

"He asked me to come and I did," she said, smiling. "Let's leave it at that."

Laura shook her head.

"John's upset about a few things," Grace said. "You know how he gets. Pressures of his work. You've told me that yourself. It'll all blow over in a few days, Laura."

Laura pushed some hair out of her eyes. "It won't blow over, Grace," she said, "but I can see there's no way to make you tell the truth about why you're here. All right then. You sleep here. Help yourself to the food. Stand guard over my children, that's why you were sent, and don't worry anymore about being straightforward with me over your reasons. But if you dare complain that I'm not being nice enough to you, then you'd better start thinking about protecting yourself."

Her hands folded in her lap, Grace sat a long time looking up at her. Finally she cleared her throat very softly. "May I use the phone?"

"Yes, Grace."

She got up and walked past her, down the hall. Laura heard her descend the stairs. After a moment she dialed the telephone at the bottom. Laura listened to her muffled voice as she spoke quietly below, then when she had finished, walked down the stairs after her.

Grace was standing at the bottom beside the phone. "Frank's coming," she said.

"Because you can't handle me."

"I called for his advice, but he insisted on coming over."

"Because he doesn't feel you're safe here."

Grace went past her and into the living room, seated herself on the edge of the sofa nearest the front door and looked out toward the street. "You don't have to wait with me," she said.

"Are you both going to stay here tonight?"

"That's up to Frank."

"We're lucky to have Frank, aren't we, Grace."

Grace continued looking out at the street.

"Aren't we."

"I didn't expect you to be this unsettled, and I'm sorry that you are. Frank will know what to do."

Laura watched her a few more moments. "Why isn't Frank at work."

"He brought his work home this afternoon."

When Frank arrived, Grace rose from the sofa, went into the front hallway and pulled open the door for him.

Laura listened from the other room as the two of them spoke softly. Then, followed by his wife, Frank came in. "Hello, Laura." He walked toward her, holding out his hand.

Laura shook it.

He turned and gestured toward the sofa. "Why don't we all try and get some perspective on this before any of us says anything we wind up regretting later."

Grace went to the sofa.

Frank glanced at Laura, then walked to a chair next to the wall. "Not sitting, Laura?"

"No, Frank."

"Mind if I do?"

"Go ahead, Frank."

He seated himself, crossed his legs and looked up at her. "Tommy and Flora home a little early today?"

"Yes, Frank."

He removed an aluminum lighter from his pants pocket. "I'm trying to think of the name of that marvelous third-grade teacher they had over there when our boys went through. What was her name, Gracie?"

"Mrs. Oliphant."

"Excuse me, please." Laura started toward the hall.

"Where are you going?"

"I'm going out of the room, Frank, because I don't want to talk about this."

Grace looked quickly at her husband.

Settling back in his chair, Frank opened his lighter, then clicked it shut. "Sit down, Laura."

"You may stay," she said. "Grace may stay. You may stay and see that I don't harm my children, as you've been asked." She turned toward Frank. "But don't ask me to sit here and make small talk with you, Frank. I won't do it."

"She's been like this ever since I got here."

Frank held up his hand for his wife to be still.

"Yes, I've been like this, and I'm going to be like this till you go. So it's best we don't stay in the same room."

"Laura," Frank said, "I'm going to tell you an incident that happened this morning at the gas station across from our building."

Laura walked out of the room.

"I can't do anything with her, Frank."

Laura continued down the hall and pushed through the doorway of the kitchen. She sat down and rested her hands on the table. In the other room she could hear the soft voices of Grace and her husband. Several moments later the front door opened. Laura looked up. It closed, then it was quiet. She got up. Slowly, she walked across the kitchen.

"Tommy?" Frank called. "Flora?"

Laura pushed open the swinging door. At the bottom of the stairway, Frank was looking up at Flora, on the landing above. "What's the show?"

Flora said something Laura couldn't hear.

"I'll be down here, dear, if you need anything," Frank said. "Just come on down."

Flora returned up the stairs.

Laura watched as Frank walked slowly back into the living room and seated himself. He brushed something off his lower lip with his finger, then turned toward the window.

Laura walked into the room.

"Beautiful kids, just gorgeous."

"Thank you, Frank."

"I haven't seen rosy cheeks like Flora's since we were in Bremerhaven."

Laura seated herself across from him. "We don't need to be unfriendly to each other, Frank."

"Who said we did."

"We can speak honestly with each other."

"It's the only way."

"Yes it is, Frank, so why don't you tell me why you're here."

He adjusted his shoulders slightly, "Laura."

"Don't keep talking to me in this new way."

He frowned. "New way?"

"You know what way I mean. The way you've been talking to me since you got here. The way you look at me since John told you whatever he did about me. You don't want to speak honestly with me, Frank. Because of some misguided sense of responsibility you feel toward John, you've changed toward me. I can't stop you from occupying my house, but I don't have to be treated this way by you, so I'm going to tell you the reason John considers me incapable of taking care of my children. Or at least why he says he does. Because I don't think he even does feel that way. But I want you to know the incident he's using to create this confusion for everyone."

Frank looked down at the shiny lighter he was holding.

"Ten months ago, John felt he had to go to a beach party given by some people who put out a medical journal. He felt I had to be with him, that it would look bad if I wasn't, because he wanted them to assign him and his partner a series of articles for them. That's why we went.

And it happened that Flora had the measles that week, but it didn't matter, because if I wasn't with him the editor might think he didn't have a full and happy home life. So I called a friend to stay with Flora and we went to the beach."

Frank raised his hand.

"I'm not Grace, Frank. I don't shut up when you wave your hand through the air. I'm telling you what happened, and why John considers me unfit, which is why we're here. So put your hand down, and listen to me talk."

"I just don't like you to feel you have to explain anything to me."

"Well I feel I do."

He clicked open the lighter, then snapped it closed again.

"All right, Frank?"

"Go ahead."

"We took Tommy with us to the beach that day because I didn't want to leave him here with Flora. John didn't want Tommy to come. He thought it would look bad to the others for us to bring him, but I made him take him so Flora could be here alone and rest."

Frank dropped his lighter onto the floor.

"I'm sorry this is so boring."

"It's not," he said, bending forward to pick it up.

"Do you want to be offered a cigarette?"

"You were saying John didn't want you to take Tommy to the beach." He put the lighter back in his pocket.

"He didn't, but I took him along, and when we got there John was beside himself with embarrassment that I had, and spent the entire afternoon telling me what a bad impression I was making on the medical-journal people by staying off with Tommy."

Frank nodded. "Actually, Laura, John may have told me about this last night."

"I want you to hear it from me now."

"Something about Tommy being buried?"

"I'm coming to that, Frank. Don't worry, I wouldn't leave out the best part."

Frank folded his arms across his chest.

"I buried Tommy up to his neck in the sand and abandoned him as the tide rose slowly around his head. That's how John told it, isn't it."

"I can't honestly say I was listening that carefully, Laura."

"You aren't listening now, Frank," she said, "and it's because you don't want to see John as he is. That afternoon was John the way he really is. Picking at me from the moment we got there to come join the others. Nearly hysterical because some other free-lance writer there was making a better impression on the editors than he was. Bringing down drink after drink to me so I would loosen up, as he called it, and come back to the party. I didn't want to drink, Frank, I just wanted to go home. I wanted to call the house and find out how Flora was, but John didn't think it would look casual for me to go up to the pay phone on the highway. So I sat down by the water while John brought me drinks and told me Tommy and I were destroying his career by our selfishness. But he didn't tell you that part, did he."

"Let's consider the record straight now," Frank said, looking up at her.

"We'll consider it straight when it is straight."

Frank rose from his chair. "It's straight, Laura."

"Frank, did Grace ever throw anything at you?" Laura rested her hand on a book on the table beside her. "Did she?"

"Laura."

"Just tell me if she did."

"We don't throw things at each other in our house, Laura."

"Maybe you should."

Frank stepped back to his chair and sat. "You say John was bringing you drinks down by the water."

"I was drunk, Frank, because he brought me so many, and made me drink them. But when they wrote on the hospital report about Tommy that I was inebriated when the accident happened I didn't say anything about why I was that way because I knew it would have made John look bad, and no matter what he's convinced himself, I don't want to hurt him, I want to help him."

"Did he get the assignment?"

"I don't see what that has to do with it."

Frank shrugged.

"He didn't get it," she said, "but all I want to do is tell you the way this happened."

"You go right ahead, Laura."

"There was an old man fishing next to where Tommy and I were, Frank, and I should have known better, but when John began calling me to come up to the others I told the old man to watch Tommy till I came back, and he said he would."

"Tommy was buried."

"Tommy was miserable all the way down, and when we got there he wanted me to bury him, and it was the only thing that seemed to cheer him up. So I did."

"Up to his neck."

"Yes. Back from the waves, though."

"With his arms down at his sides? I mean was he in a standing position?"

"Yes."

"Just trying to visualize."

"I thought it was back from the waves, Frank, I told the old man to watch him. I went up to the others, John was yelling at me. I didn't think, it was bad of me, but it didn't seem dangerous, the waves were low, the tide must have been coming in." She put her hand up to her forehead. "If he just hadn't made me take the drinks, Frank, it couldn't have happened. I went up there. I did forget Tommy. I mean I was really, really drunk. Nearly sick. Everybody was singing. Standing in a circle. Swaying and singing, their arms locked. It was getting dark, I told the fisherman to watch him." She looked up. "I had to go up there for John, Frank. Tommy refused to come. He started crying when I started to dig him out. So I went by myself. I did forget him. I just forgot him. I don't know how I could have, but I did. All the noise. The singing. He must have screamed for me. Half an hour or so. John didn't think of it either, but no one ever says anything about that. So I was up there, trying to join in so John would get the assignment. The waves were rising up around Tommy's face while I was up there singing, trying not to be sick." She sank down onto the sofa. "A man and his wife were walking along the beach, and found him. They saved his life. The woman ran up to us, screaming that a child had drowned. Her husband came carrying Tommy, all limp, dripping with sand. Oh God, Frank." She reached up and covered her face with her hands. "There was a hospital down the highway. Someone drove him there and they revived him. Frank, please don't let John do this to me."

For a long time it was quiet as Frank sat looking down at the carpet. Finally he got up from his chair. He stood beside it several moments, then cleared his throat. "Wait here, Laura," he said, walking past her. "I think we could both use something to steady ourselves."

She looked up as he left the room, then heard him, in the dining room, opening the liquor cupboard. A bottle clanked softly as it was removed from its shelf.

"Don't get up, Laura. I'm just trying to remember what that drink was that John made for us the time Grace and I were here with our Baja movies."

Laura got up and walked to the entrance of the room.

Frank was holding a brown bottle toward the window to see the level of the liquid inside. He returned it to the cupboard and took out another. "I have the name of it right on the end of my tongue."

"Frank, I don't want a drink now."

He motioned for her to walk with him to the kitchen.

"I'm going up to see the children."

"We'll have a light one first." Frank pushed open

the kitchen door with his shoulder. "Say, did Grace tell you we went ahead with that little twenty-four-footer down at the harbor?"

She glanced at the stairway.

"I need some help finding things out here, Laura. Just for a second, then I'll let you go."

"Did you want me to fix your drink for you, Frank?"

"If you would, Laura. We call our little dinghy the *Princess Grace*. Not a scratch on it even though it was owned by the builder for two months before we got hold of it."

She walked in as he held the door open for her and to the refrigerator.

"She has a little outboard on the back, Laura, but hell, with the breeze we've had down there the last two Sundays we haven't even had to turn it on getting out of the slip."

Laura carried an ice tray to the shelf.

"There's another couple we've gotten to know down there. This fellow's retired at forty-three." He set his bottle down beside her. "Laura, say what you will, but I just can't see early retirement. Sure, it sounds good, it looks good on paper. But I don't buy it."

"How did you want your drink, Frank."

"An inch or so. That much water. Now take this fellow Carlson, he has a place down there across from the marina. Sails every day. Knows all the boat owners by their first names, and Loretta, Mrs. Carlson, just about lives there at the clubhouse, you can't go down without seeing one or the other of them coming in or out of it with somebody. But Laura, tell me if I'm wrong, but at age forty-three I don't care how much you've made I don't think you're emotionally ready for that kind of life. It has to be dull as. . . ."

"Tell me how much, Frank." She held the bottle over a glass.

"An inch or so."

She poured till he raised his hand.

"*Sixty*-three, *may*be. Forty-three? Count me out."

Laura banged the ice tray down on the shelf. "I really can't chat now, Frank."

"Carlson takes me out on his cruiser last Sunday morning, just past the breakwater. I've wanted to see how she rides. He takes me out and cuts the engine a few hundred yards out and starts giving me the story of his life."

She dropped two ice cubes into the glass.

"Not his whole life, but since he's moved down to the yacht basin he's developed a habit. A quirk, that's what it is. To hear him tell it, it's a fine art. Just a splash of water."

She held it under the faucet.

"A fetish, that's what I told him it was, we know each other well enough that I could say that. That's good."

She turned off the faucet and handed the glass to him. "I'll be upstairs, Frank." She walked past him toward the door.

"Jewish girls."

She stopped.

"He can't get enough of them. God knows where he finds them, but he turns them up at an astonishing rate, according to him. Tells Loretta he's off looking for retirement property, she's so slushed all the time she couldn't care less, so Miles hops into his XKE and tools down the coast. Apparently he's got them stashed at convenient intervals all the way down to the border, a couple up in Santa Ana and another at Palm Desert, when he feels ambitious."

Laura turned around toward him.

"He gets hold of them through these swinger magazines, he showed me these lists of them he keeps hidden under the Scotch cooler on his boat, lists of names and pictures, you write to them and start up a correspondence. But the goddamned thing is, though, if they aren't Jewish he won't touch them. He said he drove all the way to Colton for an eighteen-year-old who sent him these spread-eagle shots of herself, found out she was the daughter of a Methodist minister, turned around and drove all the way back without touching her."

Slowly, Laura walked to the kitchen table.

"I told him he'd better go back into the cardboard business if that's all he can think of to do." Frank took a sip of his drink. "No, he said, they've got a rhythm or something in the way they do it that's different from anything else he ever experienced. You didn't get a drink, Laura."

She looked down at the pattern of crisscrossing red lines on the tabletop in front of her.

"You ought to have a light one, Laura. You're going through hell. Really." He tilted backward on his chair and removed a glass and a melting ice cube from the shelf. "You don't meet a crackpot like that every day, do you." He poured some liquor into the glass and dropped in the ice.

"No," Laura said, her eyes on the surface of the table.

"Miles Carlson," he said, recapping the bottle, "he's almost worth the price of membership."

"Frank."

"Just a second." He put the glass under the faucet till it was partly filled, then held it out to her. "Laura, don't misinterpret me about all of this, I don't make these distinctions myself. Colored, Jewish, it doesn't matter to me. But this character has a real . . . obsession, that's all you can call it, about this. Because you're depressed about this stuff with John I thought it might give you a good laugh to hear about it. Don't you want this?"

She shook her head.

He picked up his own drink again. "Carlson says they're more willing, they don't have that Puritan thing in them. Who knows. Who *cares?* Laura, I haven't the time to be thinking of that type of thing. I've got a business to run and if I start worrying about crap like that I'm not going to be at the top of the pile, and we are at the top. I don't know if you read we jumped to twenty-ninth in the last register of statewide independent investment firms."

"I didn't see that."

"I can't be thinking of kinky stuff like that, but it did seem like a nice comment on early retirement." He leaned back slightly in his chair. "You think of gardening and a little travel in the autumn of your life, but something like that has to take the prize for creative retirement." He reached up to loosen his tie.

"Jewish women," Laura said.

"He tells them in his letters he has a 'weakness' for

them, that's his line." He laughed. "I hate to think what goes on when he's with them. Whips, boots, God knows." He laughed again.

"Frank, could I ask you to go out and get a bottle of soda."

"Don't worry about me," he said, raising his glass, "I always take water."

"I know, but I'd like some in the house."

"Oh." He leaned forward. "Well I'll run over and get a bottle of ours."

"I really would like a carton of it, Frank. I was planning to go out for some this afternoon, then all this came up and I didn't."

"I guess I could go out and buy some if you'd like. Sure." He got up from the chair. "You wouldn't want me to take your car."

"The keys are in it."

"I came to help and I'm going to do it every way you tell me." He took a final swallow from his drink and walked to the back door. "I'm here to lean on, Laura, you lean right on me." He pushed through the door and it slammed behind him. Several moments later the car started. Laura watched its roof passing back along the lower edge of the window. Then she went into the front hall, picked up the receiver and dialed.

"Hello?" Grace said.

"It's me, Grace. I'm calling to apologize for the way I acted when you were here."

"Oh, Laura."

"I am sorry."

"Dear, we both love you so much and it just upsets

us so to see you unhappy this way. Don't think of apologizing to anyone for anything."

Laura seated herself. "Thank you, Grace, but I didn't have the right to talk to you the way I did."

"Anyway, this whole thing will be over in a matter of hours, Laura, and we'll all wonder what the fuss was about in the first place. That's a promise."

"May I ask you something, Grace?"

"Anything at all."

"It's something John and I have talked about between ourselves. He's felt it contributes to some of our misunderstandings, and I want to find out if he might have mentioned it at your house last night."

"Go right ahead, and don't think it's a trouble, it never could be."

"It's something we were sure wouldn't make a difference before we were married, I don't really know if it does or not, John isn't sure either, but let me ask you if anything was said at your house when John was there about religion."

"Religion?" Grace said.

Laura moved the receiver around to her other ear.

"Yes, there was Laura, now that you mention it, John talked mostly to Frank about it, but he did tell us that your mother is Jewish. Is that what you mean?"

"He did speak to Frank about that then."

"Oh yes, for quite a while. Frank was very interested and thought that might be something that could be behind some of this friction. You're half-Jewish then, Laura."

"He definitely did bring that up with Frank then?"

"Oh yes, but you know I never would have thought you were, not that it makes the slightest difference to either of us. We aren't prejudiced against anyone who's different and that's another reason Frank and I can be so helpful to you, if you're Jewish, because we don't even notice things like that."

"Thank you, Grace."

"Is Frank by the phone? I don't know if I'm coming back there, or if he's coming here, or what. I don't know what to do."

"He's not by the phone, Grace."

"He's probably with the children. You know, children just love Frank. Well would you ask him, if it wouldn't be too much trouble, if he would mind calling me when he's finished with them?"

When Frank returned from the liquor store he had three quarts of club soda which he set down on the table inside the front door. "No cartons, Laura, but these'll keep with these screw-on tops."

"Grace wants you to call her," Laura said.

Frank lifted another bottle out of a paper bag and held its label to face Laura. "Ever tried this?"

"No."

He set it down next to the soda.

"Grace doesn't know what to do."

"She gets rattled," he said, walking to the phone. "She probably shouldn't have come over here in the first place." He seated himself. "What I'd better do is sack out on your couch tonight. That'll put John's mind at ease. We'll let Grace get a good night's sleep at home. She's been tired lately, Laura." He picked up the receiver.

"Could I ask you something about John's visit to your house last night?"

"Shoot, Laura."

"Did he say anything about a religious problem between us?"

Frank began to dial. "Not to me. Maybe to Grace."

"Nothing?" she said.

"Nothing to me." He dialed again. "Excuse me, Laura."

She turned and walked slowly out of the room.

When the call was over Frank removed his coat and rested it beside the phone. He laid his tie on top of it, then unbuttoning the top button of his shirt he walked into the kitchen to Laura. "She's a wonderful, warm-hearted woman," he said, "but she's got to learn life can't be a bowl of roses every minute. But she's beginning to learn. Hell, you helped her see that today. She came over here to help you and you introduced her to a little stronger sense of reality. Laura, did I see one of those barbecued chickens in the icebox?"

"Frank, I think I can take care of myself all right now, and I want to thank you for everything you've done."

He pulled open the refrigerator. "I've been so darn depressed ever since John came over last night with the news of your break-up that I haven't eaten very well. A doughnut and coffee is all I've had all day, and I think I'd better start to build my strength back up." He pulled out a small aluminum-foil tray containing a browned chicken wrapped tightly in cellophane. "I'd love to have some of this, Laura. Would you mind?"

She stood looking at him from the doorway.

"Would you?"

"I'm all right now, Frank."

He reached for a can of beer. Nudging the refrigerator door closed with his elbow, he carried the beer and the chicken to the table. He opened a drawer and pulled out a napkin. "I'm going to try to save this shirt," he said, shaking out the napkin, tucking a corner of it between his collar and his neck. "No point Grace having to do another load before the end of the week." He picked the chicken up, turned it over and found a loose corner of cellophane. "I'll just use my fingers," he said, peeling the wrapping back across the legs. "I never felt you and I were formal with each other." He pulled a wing out from a side of the bird, twisted it one way, then the other, till it broke off. "They do a job on these birds down there, don't they," he said as he pulled the bone through his teeth. "Tender and moist every time." He dropped the finished wing on the table and dug his forefinger into the bird's breast, tearing most of it off and raising it to his mouth.

"Frank, I want you either to go home or call John."

He reached under the table and pushed out a chair for her. "Sit down, Laura, really, so we can talk."

"Will you call John?"

"If you want me to, and you sit down a minute."

She seated herself on the chair.

Putting his fingers around one of the chicken's legs Frank bent it slowly downward until it tore loose from the socket. "Of course John's pretty mixed up right now. I wonder if we shouldn't just leave him alone to find himself again. We all need that from time to time, Laura. You're his wife, I'm his friend. Maybe we owe him the freedom to think the things through that are pestering him. Anyway, I wouldn't know where to call him."

"Then I want you to call his lawyer."

Frank finished the leg bone and set it on the table.

Laura leaned forward. "Call his lawyer and have him tell John that Grace isn't staying here. Will you do that, Frank?"

"I'll clean all this up, Laura, don't worry about that. I'm not one of these chauvinists."

"Frank, I want John to know you're staying here instead of Grace."

He rubbed his hand over the napkin on his chest. "You want me to tell his lawyer I'm staying here now."

"Yes."

"For a point of information? Why would we need to do that." He picked up the beer can and pulled off its tab.

"I want John to know."

"That I'm staying here instead of Grace."

"Yes."

"Well I'll certainly tell him when I see him."

"No, Frank."

"I just don't think we ought to go through lawyers and go-betweens for some technical change in who's here and who's there. What difference does it make." He took several swallows of beer.

"His name's Mr. Washington."

Frank returned the can to the table. "And you want me to tell him the change."

"And that he's to tell John."

Frank nodded. "If you want me to, Laura. Okay. You don't want me to finish this first?"

"Finish it after the call."

He pulled off the next leg. "You want me to say I came because Grace was too upset to stay?" He tore at the flesh with his teeth. "I mean I'll have to say why, won't I."

"Say what you want, Frank."

"You know, Laura," he said, picking up his beer, "let's just think a minute. Now isn't it just possible that telling John Grace couldn't stay here because of the charged atmosphere might have just the opposite effect from reassuring him that all was well?"

"Then call Grace and tell her to come back."

He shook his head. "Too precarious."

"Then I want John told. Or you to go."

"Laura, I'd have to give him some reason why you're having me call. And I don't really think there is one."

Laura looked down at the pile of bones.

"You apparently feel something about my presence here that makes it different than if it were Grace." He shrugged. "Who knows, maybe in your state of mind you might even infer I was having thoughts I shouldn't be having about you. That's possible, and even understandable, Laura, under the stress you're experiencing now. But I just don't think we want to alarm John by presenting it all to him in a way that could convey that these misgivings were real."

She watched as he put his forefinger into his mouth and pulled it out again.

"Didn't you see John's lawyer this morning?" Frank said.

"Yes."

"But you don't want to call him yourself."

"No."

"May I ask why you don't want to do it yourself?" She shook her head.

"He wasn't unreasonable, was he."

"He was reasonable."

"These lawyers can be very overbearing sometimes."

"No, he thought I was crazy," she said quietly, getting up from her chair. "Like you do."

Frank frowned.

"I'll be upstairs."

"I'm not sure I caught what you just said, Laura."

"You caught it, Frank." She turned toward the door, but Frank rose from his chair and reached for her arm.

"Get your hand off me."

He kept his fingers around the upper part of her arm. "You're misinterpreting a gesture of friendship, Laura."

"Take your hand off."

"I want to help." He lowered his hand. "That's all."

"Keep away from me, Frank."

"This hurts me."

She glanced down at the grease marks on her arm. "I'm sorry it hurts you, but if you come upstairs, or even on the stairs, any time while you're here, I'll start screaming through the window and I won't stop." She hurried out of the kitchen.

$\mathcal{T}$HE DOOR of Roger Pardee's office was ajar the next morning when Laura arrived. She pushed it the rest of the way open and he looked up from some papers on his desk. "Laura."

"I just want to know if you've seen John, Roger. I came to find out if you've talked to him or seen him."

"Come in, Laura."

"Please tell me if you have."

"Yes, I have."

"Today?"

"Yes, at the coffee shop downstairs."

"Do you know why he's doing this to me, Roger?"

He looked at her a few moments, then opened a small briefcase on the desk beside the papers. "I have to buy a pair of shoes, Laura. Come with me and we'll talk."

"He met you at the coffee shop because he was afraid I might come up here and find him. Is that right?"

He placed the papers in the case. "Laura, we're trying to get one of the aviation magazines to run a series of articles on a new engine we've been watching. John brought these papers over for me to take along to a presentation this morning." He closed the case.

"Roger, will you tell me where he is?"

"He didn't say where he's staying."

"Do you think it's fair that he doesn't even let me talk to him?"

"No."

"You don't."

"I don't feel it is."

"And did you tell him that?"

He pressed a button at the base of the small lamp on the desk. "He said that his personal problems don't fall in the area of our partnership."

"Are you seeing him again today?"

"Laura," he said, lifting up his briefcase, "I can't tell John what to do. I do feel John's wrong. He's handling the whole thing very stupidly. But I'm his business partner, and I can't influence him outside of that."

"We've had you to the house, Roger."

"I know that."

"And we've been to yours."

"Yes, and Marion and I both enjoyed those times a great deal. But you're asking something that I can't do." He dropped a paper clip into an empty wastebasket beside the desk.

"Can I just tell you one thing to tell him? He arranged for Grace Crawford, who lives behind us, to stay overnight so he'd feel better about leaving me with the children. But she left, and her husband Frank came and began making passes at me. I had to have the children in bed in our room and lock the door to feel safe, and even then I didn't sleep more than a few minutes. If you could just tell John that, maybe he'd see what he's doing."

"I'll tell him if you'd like," he said, going to the door, "but it won't make a difference." He gestured for her to go out into the hall.

"Would you call him and tell him now, Roger?"

They walked down to a small elevator and Roger reached out to press the button. "Laura, you don't want me to tell you I can help you if I can't."

"But you did talk about this this morning with him."

"For two minutes."

"Can you tell me what he said?"

The elevator doors opened and they stepped inside.

"I told him he looked tired. He apologized for not giving full time to the writing."

"He's trying to get the children," she said as they started down.

"He went into that."

"Roger, I don't have anyone else that I can talk to about this. *Anyone.*"

"He said he felt badly that the kids were still with you. He said he felt irresponsible to be leaving them with you. I told him I thought that was the dumbest thing I'd ever heard him say."

"And what did he say."

"He said I didn't know the whole story. Look, Marion told me about your talk with her the night you came to the house, but this just isn't the kind of thing you can ask other people to get involved in."

"Roger, I had to talk to someone."

The elevator stopped, its doors opened, but then closed again without anyone getting on.

"Did Marion tell you the whole conversation?"

"She said you asked her to find out from me if I knew if John was seeing someone because he'd been coming in at five and six in the morning."

"But that was before I found out what it was. It wasn't another woman. He goes to men's baths."

"Laura."

"That's what it was, Roger. I went over there Friday night and they took me through them. I couldn't believe, Roger, what those men were doing in there."

"Laura," he said, "Marion is still upset about your going up to her like that. Men's baths just isn't something I know about, or want to know about. We're simple people, we're not used to all this."

"*I'm* not used to it."

The elevator stopped and the doors opened. "Do you remember down at the beach ten months ago with the medical people?" she said as they stepped out.

"The accident."

"It was a terrible thing, but it *was an accident*. Now he's trying to make it out like it was my fault. And the thing that happened in the department store last fall. He's bringing that up. But I just think he's overworked, Roger, and I want to talk to him."

"Turn down here, Laura, there's a shoe store in the building."

"Let's get together at your house. Just to talk, and relax. Marion, and us, and you. This lawyer's got ahold of him, Roger. Did you talk to John's lawyer?"

"He phoned me over the weekend."

"He's not good for John. He doesn't know John."

They came to a door with DAN'S SHOES printed on it. He held open the door for her.

"Will you just tell the lawyer you don't think John's right?"

A clerk looked up as they entered. "For the lady?"

"No, for me."

He led them toward the front of the store.

"He won't even win, Roger. If nothing else, I want to save him the embarrassment and the expense of a divorce case he can't win."

The clerk gestured at a row of seats. Roger took one, and Laura the one beside it.

"How can he succeed in this, Roger?"

Roger placed his foot on the slanted front part of the stool and the man untied his shoe. "I don't know if he can succeed or not. Something with a crepe sole, if you have it."

"How can he."

The clerk got up from his stool and walked away.

"Roger."

He reached over and rested his hand on hers. "Can't you go to your parents, Laura. Why not move in there with the children."

"If I could just talk to him for five minutes. I mean if he's so sure he's right, why is he afraid to even talk with me?"

"He's hurt, Laura."

"This is becoming very popular," the clerk said, returning with a single shoe in his hand. He sat down and began working it onto Roger's foot.

"You say he's hurt?"

"Laura, I have to concentrate on getting the right shoe."

"But what conceivable reason does he have to feel hurt. What have I done to him?"

"I hate to be particular," Roger said, leaning forward, "but do you have one that looks more formal, but still in the crepe."

"Certainly." The clerk got up and walked off.

"Roger?"

"Laura, I just know that he's very upset, and the news he got this morning made it much worse."

She looked down at his foot.

"I'll tell him about the neighbor who made the pass at you but I honestly don't think it will make him see it any differently than he does now."

"What news."

The clerk returned empty-handed. "There's a dark top with matching crepe sole," he said, "but it's with a buckle."

"Roger."

"Laura, could you just let me get my shoes."

"It's a subdued buckle, sir. I can get it very quickly."

"I'll look at it."

"Roger, you said he got some news this morning."

"I really think, Laura, you'd be so much better off if you'd just go to your parents' and stay there till things quiet down."

"Will you tell me the news."

He reached down to pick a piece of lint off his sock. "Washington must have tried to get John this morning after he'd left wherever it is he's staying." He dropped the lint on the floor. "He phoned the office just before I got in. When I came there was a message on the tape asking me to tell John to phone him when I saw him. When we met at the coffee shop I told him. He made the call from there."

"And?"

"I suppose he's going to try to tell me that's a subdued buckle."

The clerk stopped in front of them and held out a shoe with a large brass buckle covering the front. "The buckle was larger than I remembered."

Roger leaned forward for his own shoe.

"Sir, Mr. Dan's bringing out another one for you to see."

"What did Washington tell John?"

Roger leaned back in the chair. "I just have to ask myself, Laura, what purpose there is in going into all this."

"Because you've told me this much. Now what did he say."

"Do you have a lawyer working on this for you?"

"No."

"Would you like me to help you find one?"

"Roger, what did Washington say to John on the phone."

The clerk returned with a man wearing a double-breasted suit. "This is Mr. Dan."

Mr. Dan was holding out a shoe.

Roger nodded. "Yes."

The clerk seated himself and began trying it on Roger's foot.

"Washington called to tell him they're changing the grounds for divorce, Laura."

"Changing the grounds to what."

"Who knows, Laura." Roger looked down as the man finished tying the shoe.

"You don't know?"

"Sort of, Laura."

"Well if you know, please tell me."

The clerk got up and started toward the cash register. Roger stood and Laura followed him. "I need to know. What is it?"

Roger removed his wallet and paid the clerk. "Throw the old ones out," he said.

They walked to the front of the store and out onto the sidewalk. "There's a cab, Laura, I'm going to try and get it."

"What are the new grounds. You can't just leave me."

He walked to the taxi and pulled open its door.

"Roger?"

He got in and closed the door, rolling down the window as she came to the cab. "John's lawyer turned up someone to testify he spent last weekend with you in a motel. They're going for adultery now."

$\mathcal{T}$HE WORDS MS. PLESSER, SUPT. were printed in pink nail polish on a small green card on the door of the attic apartment in the building where Paul lived. Through the door came the sound of loud laughter from a television set. When it died, Laura knocked. The television set was turned off and a woman in a blue kimono, her red hair pulled back and tied with a yellow band, opened the door.

"I'm a friend of Paul Grove," Laura said. "He's not in his apartment and I wondered how I might get ahold of him."

"He's at work."

"Well maybe you could tell me if there's a way to reach him there."

She shook her head.

"You don't know where he works."

"That's not the point," she said, "but I don't think he wants to be disturbed. May I ask your name?"

"Laura Foster. I'm a friend of Paul's."

"And you don't know where he works."

"No."

"But you say you're a friend."

"Your name's Mrs. Plesser?"

"Ms."

"Ms. Plesser, I'm in some trouble. I have to talk to him."

She frowned. "You can't be in the kind of trouble I think you're in if it's Mr. Grove."

"I just need his help about something very badly."

She reached up with a long, painted fingernail and scratched her chin. "Come in," she said, standing aside.

Laura stepped into her small room.

"You must think I'm thoughtless," she said, "but I can't give out information to anyone who happens by. Mr. Grove's a very good tenant." She closed the door. "Quiet, and neat, and very honest. I don't see him much, he hasn't spent more than two nights here in the last week, but when he's here he's considerate, he respects the building and the other tenants. If he does have visitors they come and go without a sound."

"Ms. Plesser."

"When he first came here, as soon as I'd shown him the unit, he spoke right out and told me he preferred men. He said if there was a restriction because of that it should be out in the open. No pretenses. I admired that. I told Mr. Archer, our landlord, that Mr. Grove had come right out and spoken to me in that way. Mr. Archer agreed with me that it was courageous for him to have been so frank about the way he is, and on that basis we gave him the apartment." She lifted several magazines from the seat of a chair to place on her bed.

"If you're unable to tell me where to find him," Laura said, "I'd like to try other ways to look for him."

"If an individual chooses a lifestyle of that kind it's
something that's nobody's business but his. If you disapprove of the way I live, that's your problem, not mine." She
picked up a small metal rod from beside the television set.
"That's a lesson my husband never learned. He fought it,
and now he's dead." She pushed back at the cuticle of one
of her fingers with the instrument. "I didn't go into Mr.
Grove's whereabouts with you because I don't want to be a
party to having him annoyed, but I do know where to
reach him." She pressed back another cuticle. "What do
you want with him."

"I need to straighten something out."

"He's a reserved man. I respect that. What do you
want to straighten out."

"A problem's come up in my marriage."

She returned the cuticle instrument to the table.

"It has to do with my husband and me."

"If it was about your marriage, I assumed it was
about you and your husband. What is it."

"I didn't really want to take up your time with all
the details," Laura said, "but my husband's left me, and
there's a way Mr. Grove can help."

Ms. Plesser looked down at a round throw rug between them. "Mrs. Foster, don't ever think you're taking
up my time if you need help."

Laura nodded.

"I don't care if we've known each other five minutes
or five years. When you're with me, don't talk about time."
She sat down in the chair where the magazines had been.
"Manton ran a candy store over by the high school for

twenty-eight years. Right there at the end of that row of stores as you come out of the front of the school."

"I don't live in this neighborhood, Ms. Plesser."

Ms. Plesser pointed toward the wall. "Down across from the new gym. Next to Truman Hall."

"Oh yes."

"Manton ran the little shop on the corner, back when it was a candy store. It's a bike shop now. But he couldn't adjust." She pulled her kimono more tightly across her chest. "I've always been tuned in to things, Mrs. Foster, that's just the way I am, but not Manton. He couldn't adjust to the kids. He couldn't accept them after they started to be the new way."

"My husband's trying to take my two children away from me, Ms. Plesser. I have to see Mr. Grove."

"What it was," she said, leaning back in the chair, "is what we've come to call the sexual revolution. Manton just couldn't see it. The girls coming into the shop. Talking dirty, that's what he called it. You couldn't talk to Manton about liberation. To him it was just talking dirty." She shook her head. "No, the man couldn't handle change. God bless him, he couldn't keep up. Well, we buried him in his family plot. Youngest of eight, that's why he had so little ambition. I love him and I always will. But his head never quite got turned around the right way and in the end that was what killed him." She pointed at a cigarette pack on the television set. "Hand me those."

Laura handed it to her. She removed a narrow cigarette and lit it. "How old are you, Laura."

"Thirty-two."

"And you're in a divorce."

"Yes."

"You'll see three or four more before you're through. You're too young to let it get you down." She took a deep drag from the cigarette. "I'll be fifty-one next year. Would you have guessed? Pretend you don't know. How old would you have guessed if I hadn't told you."

"I don't know. Forty?"

Ms. Plesser laughed, coughed once, and leaned forward to tap her cigarette ash into a dish on the television set. "Manton always wanted children. Some women aren't cut out for that. Manton couldn't understand. I used to enter all the local beauty pageants where I grew up and take first or second place every time. If you have a figure that's right you can take a lifelong pride in it. You don't need kids. Look." She pulled down the edge of her kimono, exposing a breast. "You don't have to sag at my age."

Laura looked at the woman's bosom.

"Manton couldn't understand why I wouldn't have kids. Men can't understand. Let your husband have the kids." She reached over and ground out the cigarette.

"Will you tell me where Mr. Grove works."

"I still can't go outside without getting looks. I don't have the kind of body that can take a lot of mauling, but I'll never have to worry about not getting looks anymore."

Laura took a step toward the door. "Goodbye, Ms. Plesser."

She got up from the chair. "They wouldn't let you see him anyway. It's all passes and special permission to get in where he works."

"And where is that."

"You know what I wish I had here to show you," she said. "Last month's *Journal*. Did you see it? *Ladies Home Journal*. Black actress on the cover. Beautiful creature." She walked to a large mirror on the wall and looked into it. "The black revolution caused Manton's first heart attack. God, did he hate those Afro haircuts. Reason with him? Forget it. An extra bone in their heel. That proves it. Can't be human. We've got a black woman in the building now. Very svelte. A secretary at a bank. Very intelligent. Tidy? You couldn't ask for a better tenant. But thank God Manton isn't here to see it." She turned toward Laura. "Manton and I had the apartment down next to Mr. Grove's before Manton took sick for the last time. When he was gone Mr. Archer came to me and asked if I'd like to be the super here, the other one moved away. But right next to your friend's apartment was where we lived for twenty-eight years."

Laura put her hand on the doorknob. "Thank you for your help, Ms. Plesser."

"This *Journal* article was interviews with three divorced women. They each told of how much better it was for them without men. You should read that if you're worried about loneliness."

"May I tell you something," Laura said, turning toward her. "My husband is divorcing me. He's trying to take my children. Till this morning I felt this was a difficult situation for us all, but one that would pass if I just gave it time. But this morning, Ms. Plesser, I found out that John's lawyer has somehow got it in his head that last Saturday night Mr. Grove and I slept together in a motel in Santa Barbara, and because of that ridiculous story I've begun to see that my husband may have a chance of convincing some people to believe I shouldn't be allowed to have my children. Children who I love, Ms. Plesser, and who may have hurt my figure, by my having them, but who I love anyway. And there is no one else besides myself and Mr. Grove who even knew we'd gone to Santa Barbara together. So I want very badly to find out how my husband's lawyer was given that information. But I'm not going to take up any more of your time. Just come out and tell me if you won't help me, because if you won't, I want to go."

Ms. Plesser reached up behind her head and untied the yellow band. "I don't see why you say I don't want to help you."

"Will you tell me where he works?"

She pulled her hair back again and tied it in a ponytail. "I don't think you're very aware of certain things, Mrs. Foster. I'd expect a person of your age to be more tuned in."

"Ms. Plesser, I'm tuned in."

"Not to the Sisterhood. Or you'd realize I'm going to help you. But you can't let yourself feel so upset by the prospect of your husband getting custody of the children."

"Goodbye." Laura turned around and opened the door.

"Mr. Grove works in a movie studio."

Laura stopped.

"The men are taking the children now," the woman said. "I'm trying to tell you. The changes. The men are taking over the mothers' roles. You shouldn't worry about it."

Laura stepped back into the room. "What movie studio."

"Just this morning, before you came, I wish you'd been here to see it, eight women sitting in a circle on the floor talking freely about their feelings toward menopause."

Laura frowned. "Here?"

"No, Channel Four. But the reason, it comes out, that we have neuroses about menopause is the male's attitude toward our bodies. You see, it's the male who thinks we're useless after we pass childbearing age. We don't feel that way at all. You don't seem aware of these things."

"What movie studio does he work at."

"I could tell you," she said, "but then you'd leave. What am I to you? You come up here for Mr. Grove. You tell me your husband's lawyer says you had an affair with him. Then you let it slip you did go to Santa Barbara with him. What am I to think?"

"If it's important, Ms. Plesser, we were up there so he could take pictures of someone's house. We went to a motel so he could be there the next morning to take some pictures of the town as the sun was coming up. Then we drove back."

"And nothing happened in the motel."

"No."

"Not that it would with him. But even if it did, you're too worried about it."

"Will you tell me which studio, Ms. Plesser."

"You're having a guilty reaction to something that's accepted now in the society, I'm just saying hypothetically that it did happen, I realize you contend it didn't. And I'm not going to ask you what you were doing with him up there in the first place because that's your business. But you're as bad as Manton. Everybody's doing what your husband's lawyer thinks you did." She sat down again and pointed at a small bottle on the window sill. "Hand me that."

"Ms. Plesser, the reason I have to find Paul is to learn how Mr. Washington got hold of the story about Santa Barbara, because part of it is true."

Ms. Plesser reached for the bottle on the window sill and unscrewed its top. She began painting a clear liquid onto her thumbnail with a tiny brush coming down out of the cap.

"But there's something else I have to know too," Laura said. "I have to try to find out if John's had relations with other men. He was at a homosexual club that Mr. Grove belongs to and I would like to find out what he did there."

Ms. Plesser shook her head and started on a new nail. "He won't get the children if he had relations."

"I know. And that's why I have to find out."

"You won't lose your children, Mrs. Foster."

"But I have to find out."

"You find out and tell the lawyer. That'll be the end of it for him."

"I love my husband," Laura said. "I don't think he knows what he's doing right now. But this may be the only way I can put a stop to it."

Ms. Plesser leaned closer to study one of her nails. "Your husband didn't have relations with Mr. Grove, did he."

"I don't believe so."

She screwed the top back on the tiny bottle. "I'm going to tell you where he works, Mrs. Foster. I'm telling you because I like you and I want to see you get an even break in life. He works at the Paramount studios." She handed her the bottle.

"Paramount?"

"He's told me the title of his job. I can't recall it exactly. They send him out to scout the locations of some of their movies, but I think he's at the studio most of the time."

Laura set the nail polish on the television.

"That's it then," Ms. Plesser said.

Laura got up from the bed.

"You'll go now."

"I'll go and try to find him."

"That's fine." She smiled.

"Is something wrong?"

"Oh no."

Laura frowned.

"You go do your business. You've got your information. You go ahead with it now." She reached down for a copy of *TV Guide* on the floor.

"Well I won't go if something's bothering you."

"I can get by." She opened the small magazine in her lap. "I have no worries." She turned to the center of the magazine.

"You what?"

"Don't think to ask me about my problems. I have none. Everything's fine for me. You have a husband trying to take your children. But I'm perfect. No cares." She reached over and turned the knob on the television set.

"Ms. Plesser, I'm not going to sit here coaxing you. If you want to tell me something, tell me."

Onto the screen of the television came the picture of a woman sitting in a chair talking to another woman seated beside her on a sofa.

"I don't want to watch television with you, but if you have something you feel I could help by listening to, then please say it."

"Mr. Archer," she said, getting up, walking to a small dormer window that looked out on the top of a tree.

"Yes?"

"He owns seven buildings, one of them a large office building," she said. "He's in real estate. He's very wealthy. I've never seen his home but I know it's in Bel Aire and very nice."

Laura looked at the faintly etched shadow of a flower on the back of her kimono. "He's wealthy, yes."

Ms. Plesser continued looking out at a branch of the tree.

Laura glanced at a clock on the bureau, then at the woman again. "Ms. Plesser."

"Don't you see?" She turned around. A tear had rolled down her cheek.

"Something about Mr. Archer?"

"*Yes.*"

"He lives in Bel Aire. Yes."

"Do you think I'm the superintendent here?"

"I thought so."

She walked to the bed and sat down. "Sure, I'm the superintendent all right." She pulled up part of a violet sheet and dabbed it at her eyes.

"You're not the superintendent?"

"Sure, I'm the superintendent."

Laura frowned down at the woman as she dried her cheek on the sheet.

"Do you want to see what I am, Mrs. Foster? Go and open the drawer." She pointed at her bureau. "Bottom drawer. Go on."

Laura walked to the chest of drawers, bent down and pulled out the lowest one.

"See?"

She looked at a jumble of books, mostly paperback, but several hardbound, sticking up at angles in the drawer. "You're a writer?"

"I'm no writer, Mrs. Foster."

Laura lifted out a book and looked at its cover.

"Now do you see?"

"A story about a prostitute."

"Yes."

She picked out another. *Full-time Hooker.*

"That's right, Mrs. Foster."

She looked at another, then stood up. "You're a prostitute?"

"Yes, Mrs. Foster."

Laura nodded. "Well, I wouldn't have known that. I certainly don't hold it against you though."

"I hold it against myself. I'm no new woman."

"I don't really think there are new women, Ms. Plesser."

"Do you know the last time a new tenant moved in here?" she said, holding the mascara-stained sheet hem in her hand. "A year and a half ago. That was the last time I had anything to do. I showed her the apartment and she went over to Mr. Archer's real-estate office and filled out the application. Mr. Cotton, in Mr. Archer's building, two blocks from here, is the real superintendent, Mrs. Foster. He's the one the tenants go to when they want help or repairs, not me, because Mr. Archer tells them to go to him." She got up from the bed. "I live here and wait for Mr. Archer. It's all I do and it's all I've done for seven years. Manton left me nothing but his debts. I have a nice body, and a nice face, and now Mr. Archer comes two mornings a week. *Mornings*, Mrs. Foster. He doesn't even think enough of me to come in the afternoon, let alone the evening. I have to go to bed with him two mornings a week or I'm out on the street."

"He said that?"

"He didn't have to. I just know it. I knew it way back the first time it happened, when I was still down in the flat next to Mr. Grove's, not more than a week after Manton passed away. I told him I couldn't pay him the rent, I told him about the debts. He made love to me down there, and afterwards he said I could live up here for noth-ing and be assistant superintendent. He paid the debts off and then he started coming and he's come ever since, ex-cept when he's on vacation with his family."

Laura looked down at the drawer full of books.

"I try to read about it and learn the new attitudes. But it doesn't matter how many books I read, I still keep thinking it's wrong."

"I don't know why you would keep doing it, Ms. Plesser."

"There's nothing else for me."

"But you don't have to do that."

"I can't work. There are no jobs."

"You can go out and meet new people."

"I have to stay here. He wants me here. Not just the two days he comes, but all the time. Mr. Cotton always stops up to see if I'm here. He'd tell him if I went out. I shouldn't even have let you in."

Laura shook her head. "I can't believe. . . ."

"If I don't cook down in the basement—there's a little kitchen down there—I can go out to the coffee shop across from the school once in a while for a meal if I come right back."

"You must not want to go out."

"You say I should meet new people. If you knew Mr. Archer you'd know I couldn't think of anything like that."

Laura glanced at a close-in shot of a woman's face, her hair filling the screen, on the television.

"He takes good care of me, and here I am complaining about him, but *I just can't live with myself.*"

"Look, you shouldn't read all this stuff. You shouldn't believe all the things you see on television."

"I have to believe in something."

"But it's not the same as being with people," Laura said. "Would you like me to introduce you to some people?"

"Who?"

"I don't know. A women's group?"

"What kind."

"There are lots of them."

"You mean consciousness raising."

"Not necessarily. Any kind of group. There are societies of people interested in art. They meet and discuss that."

She shook her head.

"Or there are travel clubs."

"What about Mr. Archer."

"Just forget about Mr. Archer."

"What about money."

"You keep talking about the new woman. Haven't you read about women being economically self-sufficient? Find a way to earn your own money."

"At my age?"

Laura glanced at the door. "Well I don't know what it's like to be your age, but I really can't believe it would be that impossible if you set your mind to it."

"You're not my age."

"There are ways to meet people," Laura said, taking a step toward the door. "There are ways to expand yourself. I don't know what more to say. A senior citizens' group?"

"Oh, I see."

Laura took hold of the knob.

"A senior citizens' group," Ms. Plesser said. "I see."

"Any group. You said you were too old to work."

"That's the help you're offering then. A senior citizens' group."

"You don't seem to want help," Laura said, opening the door.

"You come up here, you listen to a woman's most

terrible secret, you flatter her long enough to get what you want, have a little joke about the senior citizens, then off."

Laura stepped out into the hall. "My name is Laura Foster and I'm listed in the phonebook under John Foster. Call up anytime you want, Ms. Plesser, and we'll talk together. If you'd like to come over and see me, you can do that too."

"Mr. Archer's never told me about his wife," she said, following her out the door. "But he can't be happy with her. Not if he comes to me he can't. But have you ever heard of a man being driven to another woman by his wife and then never saying anything about his wife to her?"

Laura started down the stairs.

"Have you?"

"I really haven't heard of a situation like this at all, Ms. Plesser."

"He never pours himself out to me," she said, going down the stairs beside Laura. "The one time I asked him about her he said he couldn't talk about it, he had too much on his mind. But he never talks to me about whatever is on his mind either. You should confide things to your lover so it eases your cares. He just gives me some money so I'll get new things to wear for him every so often. He's like a stone." They reached the next landing.

"You don't do anything about it. Maybe you like being treated like that."

"Are you crazy?" She was about to say something more, but suddenly stopped and looked down through the opening between the banister and the stairs. "Mr. Cotton," she whispered.

Laura looked down at a gray-haired man below. He was on his knees, running a length of cord along the base of the wall.

"God, he heard us." Ms. Plesser clutched the lapels of her kimono together and hurried back up the stairs.

Laura walked down to the next landing.

"Morning," the man said, moving aside as she passed.

HE LOOKED up the studio's address in a phone directory at a gas station and then drove there. It was surrounded by a tall gray wall. She sat and watched as a uniformed guard waved a car through the main entrance, closing a gate when it was inside.

Laura turned into a parking lot across from the studio and an attendant stepped up to the car. He slipped a yellow tag under the windshield wiper and pointed to a space. Laura parked, then got out and walked back to him. "Excuse me, do you know if they have a tour of the studio?"

"Not this one."

"I want to get in."

He handed her a parking ticket. "You need someone inside to leave your name with the guard." He started toward a small shed next to the sidewalk.

"Do you know anyone?" Laura said. "You must meet people who park here and work inside."

"The only ones who park here are maintenance. They couldn't give you a pass to the *bathroom*." He looked over at a black car against the curb on the other side of the street. "Try the guy in the limo. Maybe he'll take you through."

In the back seat of the long black car a man was reading a newspaper, while a chauffeur ran a cloth over the grillwork in front. She walked across the street to the car's open window. "Excuse me?" she said.

He lowered the paper.

"There's someone in the studio I need to talk to. I'm not sure exactly how to see him. I'd be very grateful if I might just ride in with you, if you were going inside."

"Mike'll let you in," the man said.

"Who?"

"The guard."

She glanced at the man in the uniform again. "Well I thought you needed a pass."

"They don't do that anymore," he said. "What union are you with."

"What?"

"Which trade union do you represent."

"Oh no, I don't represent anyone."

"They'll let you in then. Just tell Mike you're not here to make problems. You aren't, are you."

"Oh no."

The man smiled. "Call him Mike. He likes that."

"Well thank you."

He raised the paper back over his face.

Laura looked at the high iron gate a moment, then walked toward it. The guard was inside talking to another man. She stood looking at him till he saw her and walked forward. "Mike?" she said.

"Yeah?"

"I'm not with the unions."

He looked back at her between two of the bars. "What?"

"I'm not associated with any union. I hoped it would be all right if I came in."

"Oh boy." Mike waved for the man he'd been speaking with to come forward. "Wait'll you hear this one," he said as he joined them. "You're not what, lady?"

"I'm not with the unions."

"Is that a winner, Lou?"

The second man turned slightly away from them and laughed.

"Lady, you don't get by me without a pass. Did someone tell you to say that?"

Behind her the chauffeur was stepping back into the limousine. "The man in the car did."

"No lady. Go to Universal if you want to see stars. That's where the tour is." He shook his head and started away from the gate.

"Sir?"

He turned back.

"Please. I'm very desperate."

"You may be desperate, but you don't get by me without a pass."

"Not even if the reason I'm here is to try to save my marriage, and seeing someone inside is the only hope I have of doing that."

"Hey Lou," the guard called up to the other man, who had returned to where they were talking before. "She's not in the unions anymore. Now her marriage is breaking up."

The man tossed back his head and laughed.

"Lady, mail in a self-addressed envelope," Mike said. "Tell them the names of the stars whose autographs you want, they'll send them to you if they can. Now you're blocking the road."

Laura stepped back as the black limousine drove up and Mike swung open the gate for it.

There was a coffee shop at the end of the block. Inside was a telephone booth. Laura closed herself in it, called the information operator in Santa Barbara and wrote down the number she was given. Then she dialed the number and waited as it rang. "Who is it," said a man's voice on the other end.

"Mr. Davis," Laura said, pushing the phone booth door more tightly closed. "I wasn't introduced to you by my right name, so you wouldn't know who I am."

"Hello?"

"Laura Foster is my real name. But it was as Miss Haine that I was introduced to you. Sir, I want to apologize to you. Mr. Grove and I behaved badly at your house the other day."

"Is this the movie studio?"

"I'm not with the studio. I was with Paul Grove, but I have nothing to do with the studio."

"I wrote a letter to your producer. Did that come?"

"What?"

"Look, you tell your people if they want to use my house any longer they'd better learn common courtesy."

"Well I know that, I agree with you."

"You tell them my groundsman found papers and whatnot out in the back. The woman comes in here and uses the wrong toilet, and they go into my icebox when I'm out of the room. I won't have that."

"I am that woman," Laura said.

"Who?"

"The woman who used the wrong toilet. But I'm not with the studio. And I apologize for everything that happened."

"You're the assistant?"

"Mr. Grove said I was his assistant, but I'm not. I need your help very badly. Do you understand who I am."

It was quiet several seconds.

"Sir?"

"If you aren't the assistant, what were you doing up here."

"I just didn't want to be alone over the weekend."

"You're the girlfriend of the man?"

"No."

"Look, they come up over my house in their helicopter, call me up, send people here, tell me how bad they need the house. Only one of its kind and all that. What am I supposed to do. Helicopters scaring the wits out of my groundsman. Phoning, offering me money. If it means that much to them, go ahead, sure, why not. Think they care if I live through it?"

Laura looked down at the small shelf beneath the phone. "I'm very mixed up right now," she said.

"I don't even go to the movies. What do I want my house in one for."

"You're the one person who can help," Laura said. "My husband has left me. He wants to take my children. The man who was at your house can tell me how my husband's lawyer got the idea that something happened up there over the weekend. If I could talk to Mr. Grove, I think I'd know what to do."

Again it was quiet. "I don't follow what you're talking about."

"Help me get in the studio," she said. "If you just told them you might change your mind about letting them use the house, I know they'd let me in."

Mr. Davis coughed.

"Could you?"

"You let me think it over. Call again tomorrow."

"But I'm outside the studio now. I'm having kind of an anxiety attack at the moment. I have no idea where my husband is or where to find him. Oh, sir, I've felt so badly about the way we behaved at your house."

A waitress walked over to the phone booth, glanced in, then went back behind the counter.

"You want to get in the gate," he said finally.

"I have to."

"Your name again?"

"Laura Foster."

"Give me fifteen minutes. I'll see to it."

Mike had on a gray cap to match his uniform when she returned to the entrance of the studio, and as she approached it he came forward to meet her, a smile cracking his red face. "Mrs. Foster? You know, I tried to catch you as you were leaving before. I must have missed you."

"You must have."

He gestured toward the open gate. "It's sort of quiet here today," he said, "but sometimes that's the best time to see it. I prefer the quieter days myself. Go right in."

She stepped between the opening in the high wall as Mike followed.

"Mrs. Gurney will answer your questions and show you around. That's Mrs. Gurney there. Ruth?"

A woman in a green pants suit walked toward them.

"This is Laura Foster, Ruth. There was a mix-up before, I got her name from the office just as she was leaving, I sent someone to find her, I don't know just what happened. Anyway, she's here now. Ruth Gurney."

"Hello," Laura said.

"Mr. Davis's friend," the woman said, holding out her hand.

Laura shook it.

"Ruth's been here almost as long as I have," Mike said. "You're in very good hands, excellent hands." He turned and started away, but then stopped and walked quickly back. "Listen, about ten minutes ago, it must have been while I was trying to locate you, Mr. McQueen, Steve McQueen the actor, went in the commissary, that's the building straight up there."

"Is he still in there?" Ruth said.

"I'm sure of it. I would have seen him come out. Now Lou got to know him pretty good last summer, Mrs. Foster, and if you'd like to have a cup of coffee with him I'll have Lou set it up."

"I'm here to talk to a friend."

"Oh sure," Mike said, backing away from them. "I'll just keep my eye on the commissary door so I know where he goes next. Just in case. But you take your time."

The two women turned and started walking up toward the buildings. "I've never actually met Mr. Davis,"

Ruth said, "just spoken to him by phone. But what a wonderful, quaint old gentleman he must be."

"He's been a great help to me."

Ruth stopped. "Let's see now. Would you like to try and see an actor or two?"

"I want to find a person named Paul Grove."

Ruth looked down at the asphalt at their feet. "Grove."

"He goes to the locations and takes pictures of places before the others go up to shoot the movies, that's his job."

"Wait a minute," she said, raising her hand. "Isn't he one of the assistants to Mr. Gar?"

"He may be."

"I'm sure of it," she said. "Yes, he's on the picture they're shooting at Mr. Davis's house."

"That's right."

"Well he'd be with the others in Studio Six."

"Six."

"They're watching yesterday's rushes. But we can't bother them in there, of course."

"We can't."

"Oh no. But I'll have a message waiting for him the instant he comes out."

Mike had come to stand several yards away from them. "Excuse me," he said. "Mrs. Foster, I noticed you parked in the lot across the street. After this, just come right up to the gate, give a little toot and I'll wave you through. Did they give you a ticket there?"

"Yes."

"You just give it here and I'll be happy to validate it for you."

She handed him the ticket from her purse.

"No problem," he said, writing something on it. "Just give it to the boy and say Mike took care of you." He returned it to her, smiled again and walked away.

"I need to see Mr. Grove," Laura said.

Ruth cleared her throat. "Where would you like to meet him when he's through."

"I can't wait till he's through." She turned to face Mrs. Gurney more directly. "And I hate to be crass about it, but I don't think my friend Mr. Davis would want me to wait either."

"Mrs. Foster, let me just try to think a minute here."

Laura started away from her. "I'll find him, Mrs. Gurney."

"Mrs. Foster?" She came after her. "Studio Six is right up ahead, but I was just trying to decide how to go about getting you in."

They went toward a small concrete building hidden in tall shrubbery.

"Why don't I just walk in."

"Yes, but you see, you can't really do that. I'll have to go with you."

Beside the door of the building, a guard in a blue uniform stood smoking a cigarette.

"I'll take care of it from here, Mrs. Gurney," Laura said.

"But I have to go in with you."

"It's a private matter, Mrs. Gurney."

"Are you really positive you don't want to just come over to the commissary and have a doughnut with me and wait to see him when they all come out?"

Laura glanced at the guard as he ground his cigarette out in the dirt beside one of the bushes, then looked back at Mrs. Gurney. "I want to go in there. I want to go in there by myself. If I can't go in there, now, by myself, I'm going to go to a telephone and call Mr. Davis and tell him I was treated rudely by you."

"Let's do this," Ruth said, her fingers on Laura's sleeve. "We'll go talk to Mr. Lamb and let him decide. He's over Mr. Gar."

Laura turned and started back toward the gate.

"Mrs. Foster?" She hurried after her.

"I'm going to call Mr. Davis."

"I'll go see the guard." Mrs. Gurney walked quickly toward the shrubbery-covered building where he was standing.

Laura watched as the two of them talked, glancing at her as they did. Mrs. Gurney motioned for her to come. "Go on in, Mrs. Foster."

As Laura went back up toward them the guard pulled open a door with a large six painted on the front of it in red. He and Mrs. Gurney stepped aside, against one of the bushes, as Laura walked through.

It was a small, darkened theater with several clusters of people seated at different places in the room, and on the screen, as Laura entered, was the picture of a girl walking slowly down a hallway, her hand on the side of her face. Laura watched the girl reach an open doorway, look inside and scream. A man in the back of the room turned his head. "Run it again," he said.

As the screen went white for a moment, Laura saw Paul, seated near the front, his arm hooked over the back of his seat as he spoke to the man behind him. Again the girl appeared on the screen, walking slowly forward through the hall, her hand on her cheek.

"Let's pick it up," someone said from the back.

"Who told her to have her hand like that."

Laura moved slowly down the aisle toward Paul's row.

The girl reached the doorway, looked in and screamed.

"Again."

Laura started along the row behind Paul's as the screen flickered white and as the girl appeared another time at the end of the hall.

"Who told her to hold her hand up on her face?"

The man behind Paul glanced up as Laura seated herself several places away from him.

"Run the next one," a voice said.

"Does she have it on her goddamn face every time?"

The girl screamed.

"Next one."

Laura looked at the back of Paul's head, several inches in front of her. "Paul?" she said quietly.

The girl appeared at the end of the hall. Both her hands were up beside her face.

"She still thinks she's back in the soaps," someone said.

"Kill it."

"Kill *her*," Paul said, raising his arm and making a downward gesture with his thumb. "Kill *her*." Grinning, moving his thumb downward, he turned around and looked into Laura's face.

"Hello," she said.

His thumb remained pointed down at the seat next to him. The room went dark and the picture of a lake appeared on the screen, a small black shadow at the bottom of it from Paul's hand.

"Get Grove's hand out of there."

"I need to talk to you."

Paul glanced at the man beside her, then back at Laura.

"Can we talk in here?"

Quickly Paul turned around, looking again at the screen.

"Where's the boat," someone said. As he finished speaking, the front of a small rowboat appeared at the side of the screen and was rowed into the center by a man in a red jacket.

Laura leaned forward. "Paul."

"Hold it, run that back."

Rowing backward, the man moved off the screen in the direction he'd come.

"Paul, I have to talk to you right now."

"Take it across till I say stop."

"Shall I say what I have to say in here?"

The man rowed to the center of the screen.

"Stop!"

"Do you want me to, Paul?"

"No."

"Then let's go somewhere else."

"Who in the hell told that son of a bitch to whistle out there on the water."

Paul looked back at the screen.

"Christ," someone said, "he *is* whistling."

"Paul," Laura said.

"Who's talking in here."

The man beside her leaned toward Laura. "Miss. Please."

"The bastard's whistling. He's just chopped his mother into five pieces and he's whistling. I want the whistling out, but don't erase the splashing. Can you do it, Sid?"

"I'll try."

"Paul, are you coming, or shall we talk here."

Paul stood. Bending over below the level of the screen he walked to the aisle. Laura moved along her row till she reached him.

"His mouth looks like he's whistling, Steve, but I think that's a bird. I really do."

Laura reached for the sleeve of Paul's jacket and began leading him toward the back of the theater. She pushed open the door and walked out into the sunlight, still holding his sleeve.

"Will you please tell me the meaning of this," he said, pulling away from her.

Laura glanced at the guard beside them. "Shall we talk here?"

"We're not talking at all. You just tell me exactly what you think you're doing."

"Don't be such an ass, Paul."

The guard looked off over their heads.

"Who let her in here, George?"

"She got cleared."

"By who."

"Gurney."

"I have to find out about something, Paul, then I'll go."

"Call me at home." He reached for the door, but Laura put her hand on it.

"I said, 'Call me at home.' "

"No, Paul."

He turned back toward her. "Look, I'm sorry you got in trouble. I'm sorry. But it was your fault for tagging along when I had work to do, and if you were so worried about people getting the wrong impression you shouldn't have come along at all."

"Paul, I really don't think it's a matter of anyone getting the wrong impression. I think we both know it's a matter of you telling some people some lies."

He shook his head.

"And I need to know why, and what, and who."

Paul looked at the guard again. "Gurney hasn't the authority to clear people."

"She got it from Kaplan."

"Kaplan doesn't have the authority either."

"Do you want to know who cleared me," Laura said.

"As far as I'm concerned, you aren't cleared."

"Mr. Davis called the studio and told them to let me see you."

He frowned.

"Now I'm going to ask you my question once again."

"Davis."

"Somehow, Paul, my husband and his lawyer have gotten the impression that something happened in Santa Barbara that didn't."

"Davis would have had to go through Kastenbaum," Paul said, "and he's not here today."

The guard reached into his pocket for a package of cigarettes.

"Will you forget about how I got through the gate, Paul, and just realize I'm here, and I'm not leaving till I find out what I have to know?"

"Anyway, who told you I worked here in the first place."

"Paul, none of this is important."

"You want me to answer your questions? Then answer a few of mine."

"A woman in your apartment building told me you worked here."

"Which woman."

"Paul, all that matters is that I'm here."

"Was it the lady on the top floor?"

"It may have been."

He nodded. "It was."

The guard put a cigarette in his mouth and struck a match.

"I'll speak to her about it this evening," Paul said. "Now what was it."

"You know exactly what it is, Paul. Don't keep pretending you don't."

"I really don't. I'd like to help you if I could, but what is it."

"Paul, I'm asking you to be honest."

"I'm being honest."

"All right, then just let me ask you who you told what you did."

"But told what."

The guard tossed away his match.

"Paul, a lawyer named Washington knows we were in Santa Barbara. Did you tell the lawyer?"

"No."

"Who did you tell."

"No one."

"Yet the lawyer found out."

He shrugged. "If you say so."

"I told no one," Laura said. "You say you told no one. Yet the lawyer found out."

"Maybe Mr. Davis told him."

"I doubt it, Paul."

"Well I can't help you," he said, looking for a moment at his watch, "because I haven't talked about it, and I don't know anything about a lawyer."

"My husband's divorcing me, Paul."

"So?"

"So nothing that you say is adding up. You just finished making a comment about people getting the wrong impression. So you know somebody knows something, don't you."

"If I may say this," Paul said, "I'm beginning to get just a little tired of standing here and listening to insinuations about my integrity."

Laura looked at him for several seconds, then turned to the guard, who was exhaling a large cloud of smoke into the air. "I'd like to ask for your opinion, officer, about whether this person is telling the truth."

"Look!" Paul said.

"The officer's standing here," she said. "He's heard what you've said. He's heard what I've said. I'm asking him if he thinks you're telling the truth."

"I have no way of knowing that, ma'am."

"The two of us were in Santa Barbara over the weekend," Laura said to the guard. "Only this person and I knew about it. I know I didn't tell anyone. He says he didn't tell anyone. Yet my husband's lawyer found out about it in a somewhat distorted version, which we won't go into, yet. But based on that, wouldn't you say one of us is lying?"

"Ma'am."

"Jesus Christ," Paul said. "If this junk is so important to you we'll go talk about it then."

"Thank you, Paul."

"God." He started off ahead of her.

Laura caught up and the two of them walked across a wide paved area and to a large building. Paul went in first. Laura stepped over a tangle of black cords inside the door and followed him. They walked past a man raising a chandelier up on a rope by a pulley, past a tree which was propped up by a long pipe from behind, then at the far end of the room Laura saw a stone terrace and a doorway which were the same as the ones in the front of Mr. Davis's house in Santa Barbara. "Mr. Davis's front porch," Laura said.

Paul glanced at her, but kept walking.

In the corner, against the wall, was a replica of the

fountain, the broken statue rising up from the center of it, which had been in the back of Mr. Davis's house where they had talked before.

"What did you want to know," Paul said. "Could you make it fast."

Laura stepped over the rim of the fountain, bent down and picked up a eucalyptus pod. She held it out.

"What do you want to know."

"This is exactly the same."

"Listen, Laura."

She reached down to run her hand along the top of the canvas-covered structure. "Exactly the same," she said again.

"Do you know that I'm supposed to be working?"

Laura seated herself on the pool's edge. She looked over at the broken statue of the figure rising up from the center of the pool, playing its small mouth instrument. Past Paul she could see the boards and unpainted frame in the back of Mr. Davis's front door. "Did you help build this?"

"I don't do that kind of work."

She replaced the pod at the base of the statue. "I guess you don't think it's the least bit strange for the two of us to be sitting here like we were the other day."

"We're not where we were the other day. We're at the place where I work. And you've made me miss rushes. Mr. Gar does not *like* us to miss rushes."

She ran her finger back and forth over a crack beside her. "I even remember this crack."

"In about ten minutes I have a luncheon engagement. Are you going to make me late for that too?"

"Paul, you're aware of what I want to know. You've told people a lie about us. I don't know what your reasons were. It's going to cause me a great deal of trouble, which I won't bother you with, but I do ask you to tell me who the people were that you talked to."

At the far end of the building two men walked in carrying a large mirror between them.

"One person."

"You told one person."

"Yes."

"May I ask who?"

"You don't know him."

The two men set the mirror down carefully against a wooden platform.

"It doesn't matter if I know him or not."

"Then why must you have his name?"

Two other men walked in with a bureau.

"Did you tell my husband?"

"I don't know your husband."

"Then who."

"A personal friend."

"And can't you tell me who the personal friend is?"

"No, because I told him in a private conversation."

"Was it your friend Lee?"

"I can't tell you that."

"Elsinor?"

"It was neither of them," he said, "but if you must know, it was a person who I believe does happen to know your husband."

Laura frowned.

"I said I *believe* he knows John."

"Well, why do you believe he knows him."

"Because I think I may have heard him refer to him once."

"Could I ask in what way?"

"He once said he was going to see him about something. Look, it was weeks ago, it may have been some other John."

"But this is the person you told," she said. "So if he does know John, it could be the way it got back to him."

Paul shrugged.

"Paul, I think you owe it to me to say who this person is."

"I don't reveal the contents of private conversations, as a rule, although I have done it in your case. But under no circumstances do I reveal who they're with. I could not do that and remain sensitive to the feelings of others."

"Paul, I could drop dead here on the spot and you'd walk off to keep your luncheon date, so don't talk to me about sensitivity to people's feelings."

"Thomas," he said.

"What?"

A man yelled at the far end of the building and Laura glanced down to see them raising two walls around a bed.

"Actually, I may have told more than Thomas, now that I think of it."

"Thomas who."

He looked up at the ceiling. "In fact, I did mention it to more than Thomas because one friend remarked that if the lawyer was told it might help John and Elsie."

Laura glanced at a third wall being erected at the far end of the building. A loud scraping noise echoed through the room as a bureau was pushed across the floor. "I really don't have the faintest idea what you're talking about."

"Look, I don't know these people myself," he said, turning toward her. "I'm just trying to help you figure out how it got to the lawyer."

"Well you're not doing a very good job."

"You know what," he said, picking a speck of saw-dust off his sleeve. "You really ought to go talk to Thomas about all this. That's what I said to myself this morning after Mr. Washington left. Thomas could help her with this, she should see him. Of course he won't be here after today. Or I should say after tonight. I think it's tonight he's sailing. Yes, it's tonight." He looked at the watch on his wrist.

"Paul, amidst all this jabbering did I hear you say something about Mr. Washington, my husband's lawyer?"

"Mr. Washington was here just two hours ago."

"He came *here?*"

"Well, not to this building. Out by the front there. He didn't really go inside the gate."

"What for, Paul."

"He had me sign a paper. Well, a document I guess you'd call it. Typed up."

"A document saying what."

"I didn't read it that carefully. It gave the name of the place. The name of the manager, the address, the date, all that."

"The name of what place."

"You know. The motel. Then it said what we did, some sort of legalistic way of putting it."

"What we did?"

"I can't recall the exact wording. Just all this junk about intercourse, you know how lawyers talk."

"Whoa!" one of the men yelled. He hurried forward to put his hand on the mirror to stop it from falling.

"Paul."

"Look," he said. "You've come barging in here. You've insulted me in the place where I work. I don't know whether you think you have special rights or something, but I want you off the lot. On my way to the commissary I'm going to ask security to send someone over and when they get here I want them to find you gone."

"You're making legal statements that we went to bed together, Paul?"

He pointed at her. "You led me on," he said. "You know that."

"What?"

"And I will not be treated the way you treated me. I will not be used by another human being in that manner and then behave as though it didn't happen. So you get out of this as best you can." He turned toward a door, but then came back to her. "Take this information," he said. "Thomas Herron. Do you have a pencil? I'm giving you information."

"I don't have one."

"Thomas Herron. Two *r*'s or one *r*—you'll have to find out. He's the one who told the lawyer. You wronged me, now I've wronged you by signing the paper. So we're even, and I'm going to help you, even though you've treated me unjustly." He held up his hand. "But—if you interrupt me again, I will leave without imparting to you the whereabouts of Thomas Herron. Is that clear."

"None of this is clear."

"What I'm about to tell you," he said, "is confidential. Only four other persons beside myself know it. You will be the fifth. But I must know that you can be trusted not to let it go further."

"What is it?" she said.

"I want your oath that it will never go beyond you."

"You have my oath, Paul."

"I want you to understand I'm putting my own reputation on the line by divulging this information to you, and I'm doing it only because of your own relationship to John, and your interest in his life."

She nodded.

Paul folded his arms across his chest. "I have this thirdhand," he said, "but there's no question in my mind of its veracity. It happened over the weekend. Exactly what day, what time, or where, that I do not know."

"What happened over the weekend."

"John and Elsie," he said.

"What about them."

"They broke up."

For several moments Laura sat looking down at a grease spot on the concrete floor. "Broke up," she said.

"Split up, separated, whatever you want to call it."

"And that's what you wanted me to give my oath never to tell."

"I expect you to honor your oath."

She looked up at him. "Paul."

"Thomas took John away from him. Don't ask me how. Don't ask me how Elsie will take it. From what I know of him, he doesn't take rejection gracefully."

Laura reached out to rest her hand on Paul's sleeve. "Where do I find Thomas, Paul."

"He's leaving the country for an indeterminate period."

"Where do I find him."

"I guess he thinks John will be waiting for him when he gets back. Maybe he will. I'm not the one to say. I get much too wrapped up in other people's feelings. I told you before that John and Elsie were still together because change upsets me. My friend, who I can't name, who told me of the break-up, was in tears because he is the one who's losing Thomas."

"Where is Thomas, Paul."

"So you see why this can't become common knowledge."

"Where is he?"

"At seven-thirty a ship called the *Capricorn*, a freighter, sails from San Pedro Harbor. On the ship will be a crewman by the name of Thomas Herron. It is to him that your husband now is pledged."

DARK WOMAN and a white woman were waiting in an Oldsmobile across the street from Laura's house when she got home. She parked in the driveway, got out and walked up the steps of her porch. As she did, one of the women pushed open the door of the car. Laura stopped, watching as the woman started toward her over the grass. "Good afternoon, Mrs. Foster."

"Yes?" Laura said.

"It is Mrs. Foster."

Laura glanced at the other woman seated in the car, who was looking out ahead at the street, then back at the one standing beside the porch in a white dress and whitish stockings that covered her heavy legs. "Can I help you?"

"I'm Mrs. Gomez. May I come in?"

"What's the matter."

"Nothing's the matter." The woman stepped up onto the porch. "I'd just like to talk to you."

"Are you a nurse?"

Smiling, she took a step closer and stood looking into Laura's face. "No one's sick," she said, "and no one's hurt. Nurses make us think of illness, don't they, but I'm just here to talk."

Laura looked down at the woman's scuffed white shoes.

"May we go in?" Mrs. Gomez reached out for the handle and pulled open the door.

"Is it John?"

"Inside we'll talk."

Laura walked in, setting her purse on the table by the door.

Mrs. Gomez followed. "This looks like a comfortable home."

"I want to know what you're here for. Has something happened to John?"

"I'm just a friend who's here to help. Nurse Flye, outside, is my associate." "Nothing's happened to Mr. Foster." She extended her hand in the direction of the living room. "May we?"

"Tommy and Flora."

"Mrs. Foster."

"It's about Tommy and Flora."

Mrs. Gomez walked past her into the living room and stood in front of a large print of a ballet dancer standing on one toe, her other leg stretched out behind her.

"This is beautiful, Mrs. Foster," she said, leaning close to it.

"It's about Tommy and Flora."

"Come over here, Mrs. Foster." She walked to the sofa. "Let's both sit here. Come." She held out her arm.

"What's happened."

Mrs. Gomez took a step toward her and reached out for Laura's elbow. "We're going to sit down now."

Laura looked down at the woman's heavy brown fingers around her arm.

"That's right."

Laura allowed herself to be led to the sofa, then lowered herself onto it beside Mrs. Gomez.

"You have two wonderful children, Mrs. Foster. They're both happy and well, and you should be very proud to be the mother of such a beautiful little boy and girl." She kept her hand around Laura's arm as she spoke. "I want you to relax yourself, Mrs. Foster."

"Where are they."

"Let's lean back, Mrs. Foster."

She pulled her arm free.

"Mrs. Foster."

Laura got to her feet.

"Mrs. Foster," the woman said, rising.

"You've taken them."

"No, no," Mrs. Gomez said, reaching for her again.

Laura stepped away. "Oh yes you have." She backed into the hallway. Getting down on one knee beside the telephone, she opened the directory and began leafing through it.

Mrs. Gomez came to her and rested a hand on Laura's back. "Did you want to make a phonecall? I have no objection to that. I'll stay over here." She walked to the other side of the hall.

Laura looked at her a moment, then turned back to the directory, going quickly through its pages till she reached one near the end. She placed the receiver of the telephone between her ear and shoulder and began to dial, holding the book open on her knee with her free hand to read the number out of it. The phone began to buzz at the other end, then was answered. "Wesley School."

"Mr. Toll's office please."

"This is Mr. Toll's office."

"Mr. Toll please."

"Mr. Toll isn't here," the woman said. "Would you speak to the assistant principal?"

"Yes."

It was quiet a moment, then a second voice came on the line. "Mr. Rand speaking."

"Mr. Rand, this is Thomas and Flora Foster's mother."

"Just a moment, Mrs. Foster."

Laura looked over at Mrs. Gomez, by the front door, her arms folded across her chest.

"I wanted to take this in the inner office, Mrs. Foster. You know, we've been trying like the devil to get ahold of you."

"Are my children at school."

"Mrs. Foster, let me just try and recount what's happened here as best I can."

"Are my children at the school," she said, squeezing the receiver tightly in her hand.

"Mrs. Foster."

"They aren't."

"Are you home now?"

"Do you know where they are, Mr. Rand."

"Mrs. Foster, I want you to tell me if you're home."

"Yes."

"And are you alone?"

"There's a woman here."

"Yes," he said. "Yes. Now if you'll let me, I'll explain what I can."

"I want to know if they're at the school."

"I don't think you're letting me talk, Mrs. Foster."

Mrs. Gomez began walking slowly toward her.

"Mrs. Foster," the man said on the other end, "about two hours ago Principal Toll received a call from . . . just one second, it's written here somewhere."

The phonebook slid slowly from Laura's leg onto the floor.

"Here it is, sure. Mrs. Foster, the man's name was Judge Hatchard. He called from the courthouse for Mr. Toll. What it was, it was a court order. Now whether he'd issued it, or someone else, that I don't know. But it had been written up, formally issued by the court, you know, to have the children removed from school."

Laura closed her eyes.

"Of course the very first thing we did was to call your house, the minute we'd hung up from the judge that's what we did, and we continued to call every few minutes. There was no answer."

Mrs. Gomez rested her hand on Laura's shoulder.

"Finally Mr. Toll phoned your husband's office. A business partner answered who gave us the name of a lawyer, whose name I have here, just let me . . . Washington. Now we called Mr. Washington, who said he would be in touch at once with Mr. Foster. We hung up from that call and in fact your husband did phone us within the next few minutes. He confirmed the children were to be released to officers of the court."

Mrs. Gomez got down on her knees beside Laura.

"Approximately forty-five minutes later, possibly an hour, it was just as the children were coming in from noon recess, a man and a woman drove up in front of the building. We were watching, of course, for them, and they came up the walk and inside. They had the papers from the court, the order. After they showed it to us we called Judge Hatchard again, Mrs. Foster, to ask that they wait at least until we had spoken to you by phone. Of course you didn't answer. But I would like to say, very clearly, that Mr. Toll expressed the view very emphatically that he felt it was very unwise to release them without the presence of one parent, most preferably yourself. So you must understand that it was over our objection that they were released without your knowledge, but there was absolutely nothing we could do. They will work out with us arrangements for transportation between the place they took them and the school if they decide their schooling is to continue here, but that's out of our hands now. Flora was preparing to read an essay she'd written to her class this afternoon on Nathan Hale, and I think the whole thing's just very sad, but that's really all I have to say."

Laura cleared her throat softly. "Thank you, Mr. Rand. Please tell me where they are."

"That I do not know."

"Mr. Rand."

"That I do not know," he said again, "and Mr. Toll does not know."

"Mr. Rand," she said, rising slowly.

"We were not told."

"Listen to me." She took the receiver in both hands. "Mrs. Foster."

"Please," she said, squeezing her eyelids together as tears began to run down her cheeks.

"I cannot tell you what I do not know."

"You do know." The receiver was shaking slightly in her hands.

"Give me this," Mrs. Gomez said, reaching for it.

"He's lying to me," Laura said. "Mr. Rand."

"You weren't home, Mrs. Foster."

Mrs. Gomez began pulling the receiver away.

"He does know."

"He can't tell you any more," she said, removing Laura's fingers from the receiver and lifting it to her ear. "This is Nurse Carol Gomez. Is this the school?"

"He knows."

"We'll be all right now," Mrs. Gomez said, "and thank you for all your help." She hung up the phone.

"He knows perfectly well. At least he could say he knows but he can't tell me."

"Here we go." She began leading Laura slowly toward the living room, but Laura pulled back.

"I want to describe to you the place where your children are, Mrs. Foster." She kept her arm around Laura's waist. "First of all, there are lots and lots of other children there. Tommy and Flora aren't lonely, that's for certain."

"An orphanage?"

"A temporary home."

"An orphanage."

"We don't hear that word very much anymore,"

the nurse said, looking down at the carpet, "and that's because it's an old-fashioned word for an old-fashioned kind
of place."

"They've been put in an orphanage."

"No," she said, "they're at a modern place, a
friendly place, being watched by the kind of people whose
lives are devoted to making children happy. Highly trained
people who love children."

"I want you to go now, Mrs. Gomez."

"I don't think we should do that."

"I don't think *we* should either. I think you should."

"I want to leave knowing that I helped to make this
an easier time for you, Mrs. Foster, than it would have
been if I hadn't been here."

"And I'm going to ask you a final time, Mrs. Gomez,
to tell me where they are."

"I don't have the authority to do that."

"Then go. Please."

"I'm assigned here."

"Well I'm assigning you somewhere else now."

"Shall we have some coffee?"

Laura reached behind herself and took hold of the
woman's forearm encircling her waist.

"Mrs. Foster, I'm not able to leave till you've become stabilized."

"Is that what I'm supposed to become?"

"Because I'm a trained nurse and I'll know when
you're ready to be alone again."

"Will you go if I have a cup of coffee with you?"

"No."

"When will you know I'm stabilized."

"For one thing, when you stop asking questions that aren't in my jurisdiction."

"I've stopped."

"And for another, when you no longer show signs of agitation."

"Mrs. Gomez, let me be sure I have all this straight in my mind. You've come here to tell me my children were taken out of school, to a place whose name I can't be told because you don't have the authority."

"I'm here to help you accept that."

"You're here to inform me of it, that's what you're here to do. And you've observed that as a result of having received this information I've grown agitated."

"I would expect you to be."

"You'd expect it."

"Certainly."

"Well that's understanding of you. And now you're waiting till I'm not agitated anymore so you can go to your next assignment."

"You're leaving out the human element, Mrs. Foster."

"*I'm* leaving it out."

"I'm referring to your cooperation. Without that we can't get through this." She removed her arm from Laura's waist.

"*But you won't tell me the thing that I have to know. Where my children are.*"

"I can't."

"Then I want you to leave."

She shook her head.

"I want you to, because I have to think, and I have

to think by myself. If you won't cooperate with me by giving me the one thing I have to know, then how can you stay here and tell me not to be agitated."

"In a moment," Mrs. Gomez said, "I'm going to have Nurse Flye come in and give you something to help you relax, but right now maybe we could learn a little bit about each other's background. I was from a great big family, Laura, were you? And why don't you just call me Carol."

"I'm not going to call you Carol."

"And when we get a little better acquainted, I may have a surprise for you."

"A surprise."

"But first let's have that cup of coffee, shall we?"

"Mrs. Gomez, I can't imagine what kind of view you have of me to stand there thinking it's going to pacify me to tell me I might get a surprise."

"I'll get us that coffee." Mrs. Gomez walked across the living room, through part of the next room and pushed open the door leading to the kitchen.

Laura watched the door swing in, then out again, then come to rest. She looked at her purse on the front table. Then she walked to it, reached inside for the keys to her car and slid them into the pocket of her dress. She turned and looked through the door. Outside the other woman was seated behind the steering wheel of the Oldsmobile. Laura heard water running in the kitchen. Several moments later Mrs. Gomez walked back through the door. "I found some instant coffee on the shelf. I set some water to boil in a little pan." She walked to the telephone table, bent over and picked up the directory, which was lying open on the floor. "I'm going to tell you the surprise," she said, setting the directory down beside the phone, "because I think it will make you happy." She straightened the chair beside the table. "I'm going to let you talk to Tommy and Flora. I think you're calmer now than you were, and ready to be more serious." She sat down beside the phone. "Do you think you're ready?"

"Yes."

Mrs. Gomez began dialing the telephone. "Please don't look while I dial."

Laura turned her head.

"You're just to tell them you're thinking of them and love them. Ask them how they are, but I know they'll tell you they're fine. And be sure to be very positive about their new home. They need to hear you tell them how excited you are about that." She rested her free hand in her lap and waited, listening to the phone. "And I know I don't have to tell you there mustn't be anything said which would upset them in any way by having them think mommy wasn't happy. That's right, isn't it."

"Yes."

"Nurse Gomez," she said into the phone. "Will you get Thomas and Flora Foster. Admitted this afternoon by Carter." She looked up at Laura. "They'll find them right away. They know right where all of them are all the time."

"Thank you."

"I'll speak first, to make sure they understand, then give it to you. Come over here by me."

Laura walked over beside her chair.

"Here they are," Mrs. Gomez said, standing. "Who is this, Flora?" She glanced at Laura. "I have a very special person who wants to talk to you, Flora. Is Thomas there too?" She nodded. "You hold on now." The nurse handed Laura the phone.

"Flora?"

"We're living at another house now, mommy. Daddy came and saw us. Tommy got a pen set and he brought me a stuffed dog."

"Are you all right, darling?"

"Tommy's here, mom. He wants to talk to you."

Nurse Gomez stood beside her, smiling.

"Mom?"

"Tommy."

"I want to come home, mom. Daddy was here but he only stayed a little while."

"Tommy, I have to say something to a nice woman who's here with me. Will you stay right there?"

"Yes."

She looked up at Mrs. Gomez. "We've had the worst problem with water boiling down into the stove. Could you just take a quick look?"

"What's that."

"The water you have boiling in the kitchen. Maybe you could just turn it down."

"I forgot all about it." She walked away and into the kitchen again.

Laura watched the door close, then cupped her hands around the lower part of the receiver. "Tom, listen very carefully and answer exactly what I ask you. Do you know the name of the place where you are."

"It's a big new house, mom."

"You don't know the name of it," she said quietly.

"No."

"Did you notice the name of the street. Anything at all familiar to you in the neighborhood where the house is."

"I didn't really look outside the car too much, mom."

"Is there a piece of paper by the phone. Something with a name on it."

"There's no table. The telephone's up on the wall. Do you think we're going to come home again?"

"Tom, read me the numbers on the round part of the telephone where you put your fingers to dial. Do you understand."

"The phone number of the phone?"

"Yes."

"I'll have to stand on a chair."

"Quickly."

Laura heard a brief scraping sound. "I can see it now, mom."

"Read it."

There was a click.

"Tommy?"

A woman's voice. "May I speak to Nurse Gomez?"

"You cut off my son."

"Nurse Gomez please."

Laura looked up to see Mrs. Gomez backing through the door from the kitchen, a cup of coffee in each hand. Dropping the receiver on the floor, she ran to the front door, pulled it open and hurried out onto the porch, digging into her pocket for her key ring. The woman seated in the Oldsmobile at the curb turned her head as Laura ran to her station wagon, yanked open the door and crawled across the seat. She pushed the key into the ignition switch and turned it as she slid under the steering wheel. She moved the gear lever to the reverse position. Looking at the side mirror, she saw the woman in the Oldsmobile driving toward her driveway, then stopping in front of it to block it. Mrs. Gomez ran down the steps of the porch and to the side of the station wagon. "Get out, Mrs. Foster," she said, pulling open the door. Laura pushed her foot down on the gas pedal and yanked the steering wheel all the way to one side. The car sped backward onto the lawn. Nurse Flye stepped out of the Oldsmobile in front of the driveway entrance and started toward her. Laura's tires spun on the grass. She looked out the windshield to see Mrs. Gomez running toward her. She twisted the steering wheel the other way. The car leapt backward and crunched into a high hedge separating the two yards. Pushing aside branches, Nurse Flye reached for the handle of the door beside Laura. Laura pushed down the button beside the window to lock it. She put the lever into forward gear as Mrs. Gomez pulled the other door open and climbed into the car. Laura pushed her foot down onto the gas pedal but as the car lurched forward Mrs. Gomez grabbed the keys, turned them and pulled them out of the ignition switch. Breathing heavily, Laura looked at her sprawled across the front seat. "Why are you doing this to me."

"We're helping you, Mrs. Foster."

Nurse Flye began to rap against the window.

"Unlock the door for her," Mrs. Gomez said.

Laura turned to look at the other woman, banging with her knuckles against the glass and pointing in at the lock button.

"Until there's absolutely no possibility of your harming yourself, purposefully or accidentally, Mrs. Foster, we have to be your custodians. Now open the door for her."

"You think I'm going to harm myself?"

"Open this door," the woman said loudly from outside.

"You've told me my children are gone. You've done your job. Can't you just go now?"

Mrs. Gomez reached past Laura and pulled up the button. Nurse Flye opened the door. "Come out now, Mrs. Foster." She put her hand under Laura's armpit.

Pushing the woman away, Laura stepped out of the car.

"Who has the keys," Nurse Flye said.

"I have them." Lying across the seat, Mrs. Gomez held them up for her to see.

"Drive the car back onto the driveway, then meet us inside." Nurse Flye put her arm through Laura's.

"Do you mind if I walk by myself."

"When we're back in the house you can walk unaided."

Nurse Gomez closed the door of the car and started the engine.

"I want you to do some deep-breathing exercises with me, Mrs. Foster," Nurse Flye said, helping her across the yard and up onto the porch. "You wouldn't object to that, would you."

Mrs. Gomez drove slowly forward out of the hedge.

"Are you familiar with the Canadian Air Force exercise program?" Mrs. Flye said as they walked into the house. "It's so important for all of us to adopt a sound physical-fitness program as early in life as we can, and remain with it through the years."

Laura removed her arm from Nurse Flye's.

"Do you have a physical-fitness program of your own, Mrs. Foster?"

"What's your name again." Laura said.

"Candy Flye."

"Mrs. Flye, I really don't have any faith that breathing exercises would help the situation at this point. Do you mind?"

"As a trained nurse, though, Mrs. Foster, I know that in moments of stress we often constrict our air tubes and tense up our thoracic cavity. We do it unconsciously, of course, but it does severely limit the flow of oxygen to our brain. And as a result we sometimes don't think quite as clearly as we should. See what I do here. Watch me." She placed her hands on her hips. "First I suck *in* my air." She took a deep breath. "Then I blow it out," she said, expelling the air. "Do you see?"

"I see, but I don't want to do it with you."

"Here I go in again."

"I was disconnected while talking to my son on the phone."

"And once again out."

"Mrs. Flye, I am quite upset not to know where my children are. I'm not sure they were legally removed from the school."

"See how I push my elbows back as I inhale, then let them return to their original position as I incorporate a slow rhythmic motion into the exercise."

"Will you stop that?"

"Mrs. Foster, this is the only way you're going to replenish your oxygen."

Mrs. Gomez stepped in through the front door holding the car keys. "We'll put those right on the front table there, Carol. I know Mrs. Foster can be trusted now." The nurse set them on the table.

"We're doing breathing, Mrs. Gomez, maybe you'd care to join us."

"I apologize for trying to drive off," Laura said. "I was quite upset when they interrupted me while I was talking to Tommy and I didn't act sensibly. I can see that."

Nurse Gomez, standing beside Mrs. Flye, put her hands on her hips.

"Here we go," said Nurse Flye. "Big breath in."

The two of them drew in their breaths.

"Blow it all out now."

"Excuse me please," Laura said, walking past them. "If there's anything you need I'll be upstairs."

"Mrs. Foster."

"I'm not going to breathe with you, Mrs. Flye. And if you were truly concerned with my well-being you would leave me by myself so I could collect my thoughts. You've come and told me my children were taken from the school. You say I can't see them. You say I can't be told where they are. Without my husband I don't know what to do. But I have to think. I do have to do that, Mrs. Flye."

"Candy."

"Whatever your name is. I believe I have the right to at least be allowed to think in my own house."

"But you must think clearly."

"She needs a sedative," Mrs. Gomez said.

"Oh no."

"You won't take a sedative?"

She shook her head.

"Why wouldn't you take a sedative."

"Because I don't want one."

Mrs. Flye gestured in the direction of the door and Nurse Gomez walked out to the front of the house.

"Is she going to get one?"

"Do religious reasons prevent you from taking a sedative?"

"Is she going out to get one?"

"Mrs. Foster, are you a Christian Scientist."

Laura went to the front door and looked out through the glass as Mrs. Gomez opened the door of their car and reached into the back seat for a small brown case.

"I would understand that you wouldn't be able to take it if you were a Christian Scientist."

Mrs. Gomez started back toward the house.

"Mrs. Flye," Laura said, turning around.

"You're not a Scientist."

"I have no religious reasons not to take the sedative, but I will not take it, and there is no humanly possible way you can make me."

"Have you taken sedatives before?"

"Once or twice."

Mrs. Gomez stepped through the door with the bag.

"What was the problem with them before that you wouldn't want to take them again," Nurse Flye said.

"There was no problem."

"They tasted bad?" She nodded at Mrs. Gomez.

"I am not taking that."

"I just asked you, after taking them before, why didn't you want to again."

Nurse Gomez unzipped the case and removed a small bottle.

"Are you telling me you have the right to force me to take that?"

Mrs. Gomez removed a small white plastic spoon.

"In other words," Mrs. Flye said, "you don't want to tell me what there was in your previous sedation experiences that resulted in your present attitude."

"It has nothing to do with the previous ones."

Mrs. Flye walked over to the other nurse, took the bottle and looked at its label. "Just a spoonful to start," she said, handing it back.

"Mrs. Flye," Laura said.

"You relax, Mrs. Foster. We understand."

"You do not understand. Because if you did, you would know there is no power in heaven or earth that will get that in my mouth."

Mrs. Gomez unscrewed the cap of the bottle.

"You'll hardly notice that you've taken it."

Carefully, Mrs. Gomez poured some thick yellow liquid into the spoon till it was full.

"This won't make you go to sleep, Mrs. Foster."

"It will calm me."

"Yes."

"But I'm already calm."

"It's a mild, mild sedative."

"I seem uncalm to you because of what I did with the car," Laura said. "I apologize for that again. I had a reaction when someone broke in on my phonecall to

Tommy. I acted hysterically. I regret acting hysterically. I'm ashamed that I did. I understand why you think I am in need of sedation. But I'm not. Because I recognize that I did something that was irrational. And I won't do it again. If I should do something crazy again, then I think you would have the right to make me take it."

"Would it make you feel better if Nurse Gomez took some first?"

Laura frowned.

"Would it?"

"Why would she take it."

"To show you it's perfectly harmless."

Laura looked over at Mrs. Gomez.

"You take that," said Mrs. Flye. "We need to help Mrs. Foster see we're not asking her to do anything we wouldn't do ourselves."

Laura watched Mrs. Gomez place the spoon in her mouth, close her lips over it and pull it out.

"There," said Mrs. Flye.

"Why did you have her do that."

"Oh I see," said Mrs. Flye. "You think I'd have *her* do it, but I wouldn't do it myself."

"That has nothing to do with it."

Nurse Flye smiled at Mrs. Gomez. "Pour another spoonful, Carol."

Mrs. Gomez tipped the bottle over the spoon till the thick liquid had filled it again. Then she carried it to Mrs. Flye.

Laura watched as Mrs. Flye raised it to her mouth and drank it. "See?"

Laura shook her head.

"Well let's do this," Mrs. Flye said. "Carol and I will be in the living room. You think about it and if you decide you'd like some, you come and join us." She turned and walked into the room with the spoon. "We're not here to put pressure on you, Mrs. Foster. Quite the opposite." Carrying the bottle, Mrs. Gomez followed. They walked to the sofa, Mrs. Flye seated herself at one end and Mrs. Gomez sat beside her. Laura watched as Mrs. Gomez took the spoon and began to fill it. Then she turned and started up the stairs.

"Mrs. Foster?"

"I'm going to call my family. I'll be right up in the bedroom."

Mrs. Gomez took another spoonful of the sedative.

"Tell me the nature of the call and I'll place it for you."

"I can place it myself, Mrs. Flye."

"Do you feel I shouldn't speak to your family?" Mrs. Flye took back the spoon and bottle.

Laura walked slowly down to the bottom of the stairs again.

"You see, except for your say-so, we don't know you're going to call your family at all."

"May I ask why you keep drinking that?"

"You didn't answer my question."

"Our family lawyer is coming to my parents' home tonight and I'd like to tell them I want to be there to talk to him."

"How do I know that though?" Mrs. Flye poured herself a fresh spoonful.

"Are you saying you'd like me to call downstairs?"

Laura stepped to the entrance of the room to watch Mrs. Flye take the sedative. "Mrs. Foster, the demands placed during the course of her work on a professional nurse carry with them an extremely high degree of stress. There's no need for you to look at us that way."

"I wasn't looking at you any particular way, Mrs. Flye, but it seems a little peculiar that you're going to quite so much trouble to show me you're not asking me to do something you wouldn't do."

"Does the telephone reach in here?"

"No."

"Then why don't you write down the points for me to cover and I'll place the call." She handed back the spoon.

"Could I go and make my phonecall if I took a swallow of the medicine, Mrs. Flye?"

"We don't make bargains with patients." She turned her head to look at her.

"Even if I take it, I can't call?"

"There's no relationship between the two."

Laura walked farther into the room. "Mrs. Flye, my mother goes out this time on Monday afternoons and won't be back till late tonight. My father is hard to reach during the day."

Nurse Flye gestured for Mrs. Gomez to move farther over. "Make room here for Mrs. Foster."

"I don't have time to sit down with you, Mrs. Flye. My mother will have to phone Mr. Monroe, our lawyer. I want her to ask him to call John's lawyer before tonight. And my father has to be told. So do you think you could please authorize a call for that purpose? Doesn't that seem rational enough for you?"

"If you haven't talked to her, how do you know your mother's going out."

"Because she leaves every Monday at this time to go to an organization where she works."

"I can see you'd prefer not to disclose the identity of the organization."

"Mrs. Flye, it's B'nai B'rith, if that's important to you."

Mrs. Flye looked at Nurse Gomez.

"B'nai B'rith," Mrs. Gomez said.

Laura walked to the couch. "May I have some medicine."

They looked up.

"Please," she said, holding out her hand. "I've changed my mind."

"You don't want to use our spoon."

"I want to use your spoon."

Mrs. Flye handed the bottle to the other woman. "Full dosage."

Nurse Gomez carefully poured out a level spoonful, then handed it slowly to Laura. She took it from her, turned it around to place in her mouth and drank it.

"Make room for her between us," Mrs. Flye said.

Mrs. Gomez stretched out her legs, resting her heels on the low table in front of them.

"Carol, you have your shoes on Mrs. Foster's polished wood." Mrs. Flye moved forward on the sofa and lifted up Mrs. Gomez's feet. "Mrs. Foster, please accept my apologies for Nurse Gomez. We've been up since four-thirty."

"We were called over to Van Nuys on a pick-up," Mrs. Gomez said, craning her head around toward Laura.

"You've made an abrasion on Mrs. Foster's wood." She reached up to take the spoon back from Laura. "One of those wonderful new urethane waxes will take care of it, Mrs. Foster."

"Don't worry about it."

"Use this, Carol." Mrs. Flye pulled a magazine over to rest on the table where the other nurse's feet had been. "Maybe I'll relax a little myself." She reached down to untie her shoe.

Watching as Mrs. Gomez moved a brimming spoon-ful of sedative slowly toward the other woman's lips, Laura walked to the stairway.

$\mathcal{S}$AM MONROE was a lawyer who lived several blocks from Laura's parents. When she got to their house, it was Sam who opened the door. "Your dad's upstairs," he said, holding out his hand for her to shake. "From the sound of this we'd better skip the pleasantries and get right down to the facts."

Laura let go of his hand and walked past him into the living room.

"I talked to Clarence Washington this afternoon," he said, following her, "so I'm pretty well filled-in on things from their point of view."

The two of them seated themselves across a small brown table from each other. "Now," Mr. Monroe said, placing his hands on his knees, "an overview. In my experience the most valuable element in the lawyer-client relationship is a good comprehensive view of the whole horizon."

Laura glanced into the hallway. "Dad's upstairs?"

"He's getting the clippings."

She frowned.

"Clarence mentioned the department store episode as one of John's grievances."

"Mr. Monroe, I mostly wanted to talk about the children."

"We have to understand exactly how John accomplished getting them away from you, Laura, before we'll know how to get them back."

She nodded.

"Okay then. If I remember correctly, you went to the store with a group of women to do a protest against an item they were offering for sale."

"That's correct."

"Can you refresh my memory about what the item was."

"A collar for women. 'A leash and collar for your wife.'"

"Was this a novelty item?"

"It was supposed to be."

"And you went to the store to make the point it was degrading to women."

"Yes."

"Were you the originator of the idea?"

"No. John and I were at a meeting at the school the night before. Afterward some of the mothers were talking. One of them had an ad for the collar she'd cut out of the newspaper. They were talking about protesting the sale of the collars, I got into the conversation, they asked if I wanted to go with them the next morning and I said I did."

"You took Tommy."

"He had a dentist appointment that morning. The

store was only a few blocks from the dentist and we walked over when he was through."

Mr. Monroe crossed his legs. "How did John feel about the protest. Did he tell you not to go?"

"As I remember it he said something about needing the car that morning. Tommy and I had to take the bus."

"He didn't actually say at the time that he disapproved."

"He didn't have to."

"You knew by his manner."

"I knew it wouldn't be the kind of thing he'd like."

Mr. Monroe reached down to move an ashtray to the center of the table. "If he'd discussed it with you, do you think you would have been amenable to changing your mind?"

"If he'd come right out and said he wanted me to stay home, I would have respected that."

"So," he said, returning the ashtray to the corner of the table, "when you and Tommy got to the store, were the other mothers there?"

"Some were. It really wasn't going very well. Men were passing by and barking. There were shoppers making cracks, one of the mothers tried to tear a collar in half, but she couldn't. I forget who had called the newspapers, but a few photographers were standing around, sort of bored. It was just embarrassing."

"No point was being made about women's rights."

"No."

"Then who was it who suggested taking off the clothes."

Laura shook her head.

"Had that come up the night before?"

"No one suggested taking our clothes off. Just raising our shirts."

"In the paper it said you were the leader."

"No," she said. "Someone came up with the idea that by lifting our shirts we would get attention. I pulled up my bra."

"And that was the picture that got in the papers—you, standing there with your blouse open, Tommy beside you. Would you say you yielded to group pressure from the others to do it?"

"It was my own decision."

"And you feel it was absolutely accidental that the picture in the papers was of you, that by no interpretation could it be said, as was suggested in the captions, that you were the leader."

"I wasn't the leader. In fact when the picture came out one of the other women called up and accused me of trying to hog all the credit."

"Then you wrote a letter to the paper."

"People were writing in letters about me. How immoral I was. They printed those, so I wrote one back saying I didn't like exposing myself in public, but that a collar for women wasn't funny, and that I considered it much more immoral than what I had done."

"Didn't the press take a more or less facetious attitude toward the whole thing?"

"The press missed the point."

When Laura's father came down the stairs he was

carrying a brown envelope. He handed it to Mr. Monroe, then walked to his daughter.

"Daddy, I don't know how this could be happening."

"Sam's going to have the whole thing set right very soon, dear," he said, leaning forward to kiss her.

Mr. Monroe removed several clippings from the envelope. Laura glanced at a headline over a blurry picture that read "Bow, Wow, Wow!"

"Let's not let ourselves get too deeply into this incident," Mr. Monroe said, looking at the photograph. "It's sensational, but the real issues lie beneath." He returned the clippings to the envelope and slid it into his inside coat pocket. "By the way, let me say that I've known Clarence Washington since I started practicing and we can expect the very best from him in the way of fairness and the open conduct of the proceedings. But he's a tough man. As well as our own line of attack, we also want to be sure we consider John's general position too, weigh his side of it and plan realistically around his strengths as well as our own."

"His strengths?" Laura said.

"You have to admit he's proceeding pretty carefully in all this. He seems to have a pretty good idea of what he's doing."

Laura's father pulled a chair up to the table.

"He doesn't know what he's doing at all."

"Technically, Laura, he's not making mistakes. You have to give him that."

Laura turned toward her father.

"Sam's just trying to get a realistic way of looking at this, honey. He's not trying to discourage you."

"We're going to look at what they have going for them," Sam said, "and then we're going to look at what we have going for us. Then we're going to balance the two sides and build our case."

"John doesn't know what he's doing. He's just confused and overtired."

Mr. Monroe pushed his hands down into the pockets of his pants. "You're saying that all of this may be the result of John's fatigued state of mind."

"I saw his partner this morning. John hasn't been keeping up with his work. So I know he's fatigued."

"He's probably pretty preoccupied with all this."

"And doesn't anyone else think it's just a little odd that he feels he has to hide out?"

"According to Washington, he feels there's a danger to him to be with you now."

Laura got up from her chair. "What can he think I'd do to him?"

"What can he think I'd do to him?"

"As I got it from Clarence, John seems to have gone at some length into feelings about what he refers to as his manhood."

"God."

"I take it he thinks about that a lot."

"You might say that."

"He speaks about it."

"There may be other things he talks about, but it would take time to think of one."

"That may be something," Sam said, glancing at

Laura's father. "What sort of things does he say about his manhood."

"He says it's all he has. He says I don't appreciate it. He says the society is trying to extinguish it and I'm on their side."

"Is he ever more precise?"

"He points out comments I make as being assaults on it."

"Can you remember any."

She walked around to the other side of the table. "I don't think I could remember them because they're so minor."

"Even one might give us something."

She crossed her arms. "About a month or six weeks ago we were going out to pick up some dry cleaning. It was in the morning and Tommy and Flora were in school. We drove to the shopping center, parked, and I made some insignificant remark that we had to sit analyzing for at least fifteen minutes before we got to figure out whether it was a disguised insult to his virility."

"You don't remember the remark."

She looked down at the rug. "I think I said something about the fact that he stays home all day. He does most of his work at home, and that's fine with me. But he imagines that I wish he went away to do it."

"Why."

She shrugged. "Other men are off at jobs. I guess it bothers him that he's not."

"Have you told him you like him to be at home?"

"I don't think I go around telling him. But he should know. I think I show it." She walked back to her chair. "I remember what I said in the car that set it off. I suggested while we were at the shopping center that he could get another fish to keep Henry company."

"Henry's their goldfish," Laura's father said.

"I'm trying to show that what he's doing now with the children, and the divorce, is just another of the unreasonable things he's started to do lately."

"I think I understand that, Sam," Laura's father said.

"Did he accuse you of having a purpose other than obtaining the fish when you told him to buy it?"

"I would say so."

"That you were slurring his manhood."

"Yes."

"And this led to the discussion of his working at home."

"That's right."

Sam inserted a finger in his ear and began jiggling it back and forth.

"Did he buy the goldfish?" Laura's father said.

"No."

"Laura," Sam said, "possibly we can establish John's state of mind through enough incidents of that sort, but there's something no one's talked about yet. I think it goes without saying that you know what I'm referring to."

"It goes without saying."

Laura's father frowned.

"And it also goes without saying that this is what we're here to talk about."

"I won't dignify it by discussing it."

"Either to deny it or confirm it."

"That's correct."

"What's this," her father said.

"By refusing to deny it," Mr. Monroe said, "you realize you raise the question of your honesty." He turned to Laura's father. "This is the point that precipitated the court order. She can't afford this attitude toward it."

"I won't discuss it."

"Will you allow it to be discussed in your presence," Sam said.

She kept her eyes fixed on the wall, just below where it met the ceiling. "I can't tell you what to talk about, but I will not recognize the subject as one that is serious."

"The courts recognized it as one that was serious enough to have you declared unfit, Laura."

"If the courts," Laura said quietly, grasping the arm of the chair with her hand, "are so stupid as to believe any nonsensical story anyone cares to bring them, then that is their problem, Mr. Monroe, not mine."

"Laura."

"I will leave this room before I'll talk about it."

Sam reached over and rested his hand on hers. "All right." He cleared his throat. "All right, Laura." He turned to her father. "There was an alleged incident between Laura and another man in Santa Barbara over the weekend."

"There was no incident in Santa Barbara," she said looking at him.

"I wasn't attempting to draw you into the conversation, Laura."

"I don't know what this is," Mr. Wells said, "but you aren't letting the record be set straight, dear."

"There's no record *to* set straight."

Sam raised his hand. "Clarence made two phone-calls before he took the matter before the judge. He spoke to a motel manager and to an elderly gentleman in Santa Barbara named Davis. They confirmed, by description, both of clothing and appearance, which was checked out with John, that Laura was there and spent the night with the individual in question. There are eyewitnesses to the two of them being there and registering at the motel."

Mr. Wells glanced at his daughter.

"This was adequate corroborative testimony, in the opinion of the judge, to issue an unfit status to her and order child separation. And of course there was a sworn, witnessed deposition by the man who was with her that relations occurred."

She shook her head.

"You say he's lying."

"Of course he's lying."

"Well that's what we have to establish," Sam said.

"Were you at Santa Barbara with this man?" her father said.

Laura got up from her chair. "What is this?"

"Just tell us," Sam said, "in your own words, Laura, why you went up there."

"Because I didn't know what to do. John was gone. I didn't want my mother and father to know there was trouble between us so I didn't want to come back here and get the children. I also didn't want to go home alone and sit there two days by myself."

"Who was this man."

"I went to a bath club," she said, "to try and find John. His name is Paul Grove and he said he'd try to help me find him."

"What's a bath club," her father said.

"This is a delicate thing to pursue here in the family home, Lloyd, but I do think we need to."

"Turkish baths?"

"Why Santa Barbara, Laura?" Sam said.

"He was going up there to do some photography."

"And why the motel?"

"He had to stay over to get pictures the next morning."

Sam frowned. "Don't you think it's a little odd to stay in the same room of a motel with him?"

"It's odd," she said.

"You do see that it seems odd."

"Yes."

"And you're aware of the obvious conclusions to be drawn from it."

"Of course, but I don't see why there should be any difficulty in refuting a lie."

"There sometimes is, Laura. May I ask if the subject came up between the two of you about anything beyond just getting a good night's sleep?"

"He brought it up and I told him it was preposterous."

"Did he pursue the subject in any aggressive way once you'd expressed that opinion?"

"He didn't," she said. "He's a homosexual."

"You spent Saturday night in a motel with a homosexual?" her father said.

"That's another element we need to get into about all this, Lloyd."

Mr. Wells looked up at his daughter. "This family's never had anything to do with homosexuals," he said.

"All right," Sam said, holding up his hand toward Laura, "before we get sidetracked, I'm going to set forth the position. The starting point. Now they're going to say you're an irresponsible girl." He glanced again at Mr. Wells. "Before you came down we were talking about keeping an overview in all this. If we bog down on our feelings about different minorities, we'll be here all night. Now." He placed his finger on the table. "For their hard evidence against you, Laura, they're going to go into the time Tom almost drowned at the beach with you a few yards away. They're going to say you stripped in public in view of your son with the news photographers' bulbs popping. They're going to get your former psychiatrist to testify you broke off treatment and wouldn't return even though he repeatedly urged you to do so. They're going to say the mental strain of living with you got so much for your husband that he had to clear out to keep his sanity. Then they're going to say the minute he was out of the house you were up in a motel in Santa Barbara and they're going to produce a man who apparently will say under oath he was with you." He turned again to Laura's father. "Lloyd, you correct me if I'm wrong, but even from the layman's point of view, I think we'd have to say this case isn't a piece of cake." He looked back at Laura. "And I don't mean any disrespect in this to you, but I'm not inclined to go up against all that firepower and tell the judge John refused to buy a goldfish on a trip to the dry cleaners."

Laura looked down at the pink ashtray on the table. "Thank you for taking the time to see me, Mr. Monroe. I really do appreciate it."

"Well we aren't through, I'm just saying it's tough."

"Daddy," she said, "thank you."

"I painted it black," Sam said, "so we'd know where we are."

"I know where I am. I came here to see if Mr. Monroe could get my children back tonight. Tomorrow at the latest. I can see he can't."

Laura walked out of the room.

"No one could," her father said, going after her.

"Then I'll do what I have to. I'll go see a man who knows where John is."

"Excuse me," Sam said, walking in to where they were standing, "this wouldn't be the man who made the charge."

"No."

"I'm sure you wouldn't be foolish enough to have anything to do with him," Sam said.

"This isn't a homosexual you're going to see," her father said.

"He may be, but that has nothing to do with it."

Sam reached past her and turned the lock in the knob of the front door.

"Mr. Monroe," she said, facing him, "they're not your children." She looked at her father. "And they're not yours."

"But they won't be yours either if you don't settle down."

"They aren't mine now, Mr. Monroe."

"If there's something about John and homosexuals," her father said, "then the three of us need to sit down and get into it."

"You believe this man you're going to see will take you to John," Sam said.

"Yes."

"And if he doesn't?"

"He will."

"Give me his name. We'll arrange a meeting with him in my presence tomorrow."

"He won't be here after tonight." Laura was shaking slightly as she spoke. "But even if he was I wouldn't give it to you, because I think John needs me. Can you understand that? Can either of you understand that? He's finally found a way to show me he needs me. And unless one of you has anything more to say, I will ask you to let me go to him now." She turned the lock in the knob of the door.

"Laura," Sam said.

"Do you have anything more to say about getting Tommy and Flora back to me or not."

"We can petition for their return," he said, "not that I think we should at this point. I'll certainly talk to the judge in the morning. I'll put in for a review of the court order."

Laura opened the door. "Goodnight," she said, walking outside.

Her father came after her. "Sam's trying to help you, dear."

"I know he is."

"If anyone can get you out of this, he will, Laura."

She walked down the driveway and opened the door of her car.

"But apart from that," he said as she turned on the headlights, "your mother and I won't get through the night thinking of you going off to keep an appointment with a homosexual."

"You'll get through it." She turned on the engine and drove away.

$\mathcal{J}T$ _WAS_ seven-thirty when she reached the harbor. Bright lights shone across the front of the pier building and on the traffic moving back and forth in the street. She stopped when she came even with the entrance and began opening the door of the car but a policeman yelled at her from the center of the street. She drove forward. A large truck backed past her. Behind her a car honked and she drove forward again, the hood of her car moving under the tailgate of a truck ahead. She heard the policeman's whistle, and two men carrying large cloth bags past her shouted in her window. She glanced in her rearview mirror, then turned the steering wheel and bumped up onto the sidewalk beside a telephone pole. Pushing open the door, she climbed out and hurried past several men moving toward the building's entrance. The policeman turned and saw her car, yelled and walked toward it. She pushed through the door of the large building past a man in a khaki jacket.

Inside the smoky room men were standing in lines leading back from wooden tables, waiting to hand papers to men in uniforms, who sat looking at them before stamping them. An elevator behind the farthest table opened. Laura watched several men enter it just before its doors closed.

She turned toward a heavy man with a kerchief around his neck. "I need to see someone on the boat."

He shook his head and pushed between several other men toward one of the tables.

On a large white card hanging over one of the tables was a sign that read A THROUGH H. A man stepped down against her ankle as he passed. Laura forced her way between several men and toward the table. "Excuse me," she said loudly to the one at the head of the line. "Please excuse me." She jostled against him and leaned forward to place her hands on top of the table. "I have to see someone," she said to a man wearing a white cap, seated across from her.

He looked up from several sheets of yellow paper stapled together.

"I'm looking for someone named Thomas Herron. I must see him."

"We're shipping out, ma'am."

Someone shouted from behind her. The man at the table stood and looked past Laura. "Get that out of here!" he yelled. Dropping his pencil on the table, he started out into the front of the room.

Near the doorway a large crate had been wheeled partway into the building. "Who told him to bring that in here," the man with the white cap said, pushing his way toward the door.

Laura looked at the elevator. Its doors were open

and a crowd of men were walking onto it. "Please don't tell him," she said to the man beside her, as she backed around the table. Several of the men in line were watching her. "I have to see my brother," she said to them. "Please don't tell him."

As the doors of the elevator closed, she pushed herself between them. The men around her were silent as the elevator slowly descended. She looked up past a black face next to her and toward the ceiling. "Does anyone know a man named Elsinor?" There was no answer from the men.

When the elevator reached the bottom it opened on the opposite side. Laura followed the others out into a large room with a concrete floor. Carts stacked with boxes and wooden crates driven by men in gray smocks moved across it. Partway down the hall was a gate and another line of waiting men. Behind it Laura could see a brightly illuminated walkway leading up between two railings. Suddenly a loudspeaker screeched over her head. "We are still waiting for Ensign Merritt at the entrance."

"You oughtn't to be down here," said a white-haired man, standing beside her. "I saw you come past the desk up there. You oughtn't to have done that."

She looked at him for a few moments, then raised up her purse. "My brother is very sick. I have his medicine."

"Oh," he said, nodding. "Well, what's his name."

"Thomas Herron."

"Come with me."

She started along beside him, stopping as two men with large cloth bags brushed past her. "He packed the wrong bottle by mistake," she said, catching up.

Taking her sleeve, the man led her down beside the

line of waiting men and to an entrance in the gate, where a uniformed officer was looking through papers. "Ted, her brother's on board without his medicine."

The officer held out his hand. "I'll take it."

"Just give it to him," the white-haired man said. "He'll see your brother gets it."

"This happened once before," Laura said. "It was brought to the ship, given to someone, and it didn't get to him."

"I'll see he gets it." The officer continued holding his hand out.

"Oh sir," Laura said, "our mother's out of her mind with worry. After what happened last time, she won't make it through the night if I don't give it to him myself."

The officer glanced at the man beside Laura, then back at her. "Take her on."

"Oh, thank you."

The white-haired man led Laura through the gate and to the gangplank. "We can't let a man go sick," he said as they started up the metal walkway.

At the top another officer stood holding a clipboard.

"This lady's looking for a crewman named Herron," the white-haired man said. "He needs immediate medical attention."

The officer flipped over several pages on his clipboard, then stopped and moved his eyes down until they reached the bottom. "Twenty-nine D Deck."

Laura and the white-haired man walked past him. "I think I can find it myself," she said.

"You're not going on alone."

"We're a navy family," Laura said. "I just about

grew up on ships. Really." She began backing away from him. "Thank you so much. Thank you."

Following the large, lettered instructions painted in black on the gray walls of the ship it took her only a few minutes to find her way to the bottom deck. Several men whistled as she passed and some whispered and laughed together as she turned through a metal doorway and started down another flight of stairs. "Twenty-nine," she said aloud, reaching the bottom step.

A man with a white towel hanging around his neck looked out of the doorway beside her.

"Twenty-nine," she said to him.

"Cabin Twenty-nine?"

"Yes."

He closed the door behind him and stepped out into the hallway. "How'd you get down here."

"The officer said it was all right."

She followed the man as he started along the corridor. Near the end of it, he reached for the handle of a door with a small twenty-nine painted on it in black. "Who do you want?"

"Thomas Herron."

He pushed it open and looked inside.

Laura moved forward and looked past the man's shoulder and into the room.

"He's been here, but he's gone now."

"I'll wait for him."

"We're about to leave, ma'am."

"I have something I must give to him."

"Just leave it on his bunk. He'll find it."

"I have to see him."

The man shook his head. "I'll look for him in the lounge," he said, "but if he's not there you'd better get off ship." He turned and started back up the corridor.

Laura stepped over the steel ridge at the bottom of the doorway. Inside on a tight gray blanket on the bed was a carrying case. Several tags hung from its handle. She crossed the room to it, turned one of them over and read "T.H.," written in pencil under the clear plastic covering the tag. She turned over another, which was blank, then rested her finger on the bag's zipper.

From the hallway behind her came a voice. "Tom?"

She turned as a man looked in through the door.

He glanced at her hand on the zipper of the bag, then at her face.

"I'm his sister. Do you know where he is?"

The man rested his hand on the side of the doorway. He turned his head to look down the corridor, and watched for a moment as someone approached. "Tom," he said. He lowered his arm and stepped back as a short man wearing a T-shirt appeared beside him and looked in at Laura. "I've got some news for you. You have a sister."

"Thank you, Fred. I'll take care of it."

Fred continued looking in through the doorway.

"I'll see you in the lounge, Fred. Thank you."

"Check." He disappeared.

The man stood several moments longer in the hall, then rested his hand on the brass handle of the door beside him.

Laura cleared her throat.

"Paul mentioned you might come," he said, stepping into the room.

Somewhere down the hall a man called another man's name. "I regret the cramped quarters." He closed the door behind him. "You're very nervous," he said. "The sailing's been delayed for a few minutes so you needn't fear about the boat's leaving immediately." He pointed at the handbag she was holding. "May I see that? I'm a student of fabric."

She looked down at her purse.

"I don't know how familiar you are with this particular pattern," he said, stepping toward her and reaching for it. "May I?" He took it slowly from her. "It's not the standard, commercialized madras we're used to, that's why it caught my eye." He held it close to his face to examine the cloth covering the bag. "Sadly, even the Indians themselves have begun debasing their ancient weaving crafts to accommodate the popularity of this material in Europe and America. But this is very authentic. May I ask where it's from?"

"If Paul told you I was coming, sir," she said, removing the purse from his hands, "then I assume he also told you why I was coming."

He looked down at the floor of the cabin. "Sir," he said. "I know I've been called 'sir' before. Somewhere. We attach such a pejorative connotation to that form of address, yet perhaps in doing so we overlook the underlying mark of respect it was originally meant to convey."

"I want to know where my husband is," she said, taking a step toward him. "If you can tell me, I want also to know where my children are."

He frowned. "Husband," he said. "Children."

"I'm not here to waste time. Either tell me what you

can, or I'll go see your captain and explain why I'm here."

"That would be Lawrence Singer. And a very gracious and hospitable captain he is. Give me a moment and it will be my pleasure to introduce you." He seated himself on the edge of the narrow bunk.

"May I say something, Mr. Herron."

"I hope nothing I've done would lead you to believe you couldn't."

"I'm going to find John," she said, "and I'm going to talk to John, and I'm going to put an end to this. You had better understand that."

He leaned back against the wall beside the bunk. "Laura—Mrs. Foster, if you prefer us to remain on a formal footing—"

"Whatever advantage you took of John," she said. "Whatever part you're playing in all this—not that I'm interested in the details of your romantic tangles—I just want you to understand it's all over now."

"This isn't the gathering of spiritual comrades I had hoped for us, Mrs. Foster."

"Do you tell me where he is, or not."

"What a poor host you must think me." He gestured at a chair bolted to the floor in the corner. "Seat yourself, Mrs. Foster."

"You're not going to tell me where he is, are you."

Thomas looked at a small blue and white curtain covering a porthole beside Laura's head. "Laura—Mrs. Foster—you don't volunteer any guidance as to whether I should address you in a formal or casual manner, so I will employ both forms of address from now on so as not to omit the one you consider most appropriate."

"Sir, answer my question."

"I recall no question. A series of ultimata. But no question." He got up from the bed. "Even if I were inclined, though, to lead you to your lost husband, it's altogether out of my power to do so."

"You make it in your power, Mr. Herron."

"You see," he said, running his hand across the tight blanket, "the tragedy between us is that we're not talking about the same person. This errant husband you refer to, this John of yours, is gone. Vanished. Extinct." He looked up toward the ceiling. "No, the John I know is the reborn John. The John risen from the ashes of his former monotonous existence, his dull nine-to-five office routines of yesterday, and into a new day of freedom and beauty toward which his tortured soul has struggled in silence these many years."

Laura looked down at a steel leg of the chair in the corner.

"The person you seek is no more, Laura, Mrs. Foster."

"Nine-to-five office routines," she said, looking up at him again.

"Those are of a former life. Tired and burden-weary at the end of the day, coming home to an aproned wife with a vegetable brush in hand."

"What nine-to-five routines are you referring to."

"Whatever his hours were," Thomas said.

"His hours at what."

Thomas shrugged. "His job, jobs."

"Which one."

He stood a moment longer, his foot resting on a small square of carpeting on the floor, then stepped back to the bed.

"I don't think you know John," Laura said.

"Forgive me." He pulled open the carrying case in front of him. "Our chat has been so engrossing it's quite slipped my mind what I came here to get." He removed a book from the case.

"You don't know him."

"Laura. Mrs. F."

"You don't even know what his work is, what his job is."

"Well, of course he's so versatile that I know he has a great deal of potentiality in many fields."

"He's never had any nine-to-five job."

"It was another John I was thinking of," he said. "I know your husband quite well, but now I must take my leave."

"You're supposed to be his new love," she said, "isn't that it?"

He looked down at the book in his hand.

"He broke up with his friend Elsinor over the weekend and you stepped in. Do I have it right?"

Thomas cleared his throat.

"Maybe I'm being too blunt about it for you."

"It *has* just happened."

"You won him away from Elsinor. That's how it goes, as I have it."

"There was a transfer of John's affections, yes."

"To you."

He turned the book over to look at the back.

"What are you leaving for, on a boat, if you and John are just getting together."

"It's not a happy departure."

"And if you're such lovers, why isn't he down here to wave you off, throw you a kiss from the wharf."

"Mrs. Foster."

"Let's find out," she said. "You say you know John."

"He is known to me."

"And you've been with him."

"Excuse me?"

"In bed," she said. "You've slept with John."

Thomas raised his hand to his mouth and coughed. "That's hardly a subject for the two of us."

"You have, though."

"Perhaps."

"I'm not trying to make an issue of it," she said. "I'm just trying to get you to say what we both know is true."

"Yes, we've shared the joys and mysteries of physical communion."

"Then there's something you have to know about John," she said, "if that's true."

"Oh?"

"If you've been to bed with him, then there's something you'd have noticed about him."

"There are many things I've noticed about him."

"But one in particular," she said, "and if you don't know what I mean, then you don't know John."

"I may know to what you're referring."

"Then tell me what it is."

He smiled and placed the book under his arm.

"Is it too delicate for you?" she said.

"It is delicate."

"Yes, it is."

"I might even blush if I were to say it."

"Tell me this. Just for my own peace of mind. Did John say the thing we're talking about had anything to do with his reason for leaving me?"

"We really didn't discuss it at length, Mrs. Foster."

"I suppose that's a pun," Laura said.

He frowned.

" 'Discuss it at length.' I suppose that's your idea of humor."

"Oh, I get it." He laughed.

"You don't want to tell me if he talked about the times I made fun of it. All right. But just tell me if he did talk to you about it at all."

"He didn't linger on it."

"Mr. Herron," she said, stepping forward, "we are both talking about the supporting thing he uses, aren't we."

"The what?"

"The supporting thing."

"Yes."

"The elastic thing."

"I really didn't inquire as to its physical make-up."

"But he wasn't embarrassed to use it with you."

"He didn't seem to be."

"What do you call those things. I never did ask him."

"There's a medical name for them," Thomas said. "I can't bring it to mind. Prophylaxis something."

"You've heard of them."

"Somewhere."

"I'd never seen one before I met John," Laura said.

"I once knew a fellow in Calais who wore one to keep himself straight."

"In fact I'd never heard of them before now."

He put his forefinger to his chin. "Or was it the Adriatic."

"I never heard of them till I made the whole thing up."

"You know, it may not have been the Adriatic at all, now that you mention it."

"It wasn't anywhere."

"No," he said. "Well." He smiled at her. "Shall we say goodbye then?"

"I'm going to tell you something you don't seem to know," she said, stepping closer. "By false testimony, or whatever you want to call it, my children were removed illegally from their school today. By people lying to the court and judge. And I'm wondering how happy the court and the judge will be when they find out about it, and what they'll decide to do."

"I'm really not an expert on court procedures, Mrs. Foster."

"No, but you may become one," she said, "because if I leave here without knowing any more than I do now, it will be to the police that I go. To tell them what I haven't before. And it would not seem unlikely that when you return from your cruise, your presence in a court will be requested. And maybe you can explain there more satisfactorily than to me what your part in all this is."

"Let me tell you what I think you should do." He cleared his throat. "I really think you should go talk to the parties more directly involved. Let me just give you some directions, Mrs. Foster."

"I've had enough directions today," she said.

"There's something you should know about Elsinor."

She shook her head. "I don't want to hear about Elsinor," she said. "I don't want to think about Elsinor. I don't want to meet him."

"You have met him," he said. "Look, the ship's about to leave."

"I haven't met him."

Suddenly there was the sound of engines vibrating beneath them.

"You're going to have to get off the boat."

"Why do you tell me I've met him."

"Mrs. Foster, would you like to see Peru? It's quite lovely this time of year."

"I haven't met Elsinor," she said, stepping into the hallway.

"There's a place called the Grocery Store," he said. "It's on the Coast Highway, about a mile up from Malibu. Go there and ask directions to Paul Grove's house. Elsinor is Paul Grove."

She backed toward a metal stairway. "What?"

"Bon voyage, Mrs. Foster." He closed his door.

In a clean white uniform, a man appeared around a corner. "Ma'am," he said, "we're casting off."

HE WOMAN in the Grocery Store was wrapping a sandwich in a piece of wax paper as Laura walked through the door. She smiled at Laura across a wooden counter.

"I'm looking for a person named Elsinor."

"Oh, who isn't."

"He does live around here then."

"He just called a minute ago to see why his order hadn't come. Wait here." She hurried around from behind the counter to a window in the side of the store, rapped on the glass, then pushed it open.

A boy was backing a white van out the driveway. He stopped.

"Gary?" she said. "Bring the box." She looked back at Laura. "Are you going up there?"

"I don't know."

"If you don't mind, I'll just give you something to take up with you. Blackberry cordial. Very special."

The boy, wearing a white apron, tossed his straight blond hair out of his face as he carried a cardboard carton around the front of the van and to the woman at the window. She reached inside for a paper bag, removed it, then closed the window and walked back to Laura. "Don't take this the wrong way," she said, "because I really don't know exactly what happened, but Gary sort of hates to go up there after a delivery last month, I don't think much of anything happened, Gary knows how to take care of himself, but he's such a sincere kid, not a worldly bone in his body, he came back and announced he didn't want to go up there anymore, nothing against your friend, it's just that Gary's such a great, straight kid, maybe he heard some language or saw something that went against his grain a little." She handed Laura the bag.

"One other question," Laura said.

"If you want to know how to get there"—the woman pointed toward the window—"just take the dirt road past our property and follow it till it stops. It's a broken-down old house at the end. It's all overgrown, but you'll see it there through some trees."

"I want to ask you about another person too," Laura said. "Paul Grove."

"Mr. Grove," she said. "Sure."

"You know him too."

"If you know the one," the woman said, laughing, "you have to know the other." She pushed a button on the cash register. "Mr. Grove likes to be called Elsinor around here," she said as the drawer opened. "I think he comes here to get away from his other life." She lifted up a small stack of checks fastened together with a paper clip and removed one to show her. "Paul Grove." She rested her finger at the bottom. "One and the same." She leaned slightly closer. "He's in the movies, something to do with sets. Theatrical. Swish, swish. You know what I mean."

There were no lights on the road. When Laura came to the end she stopped and pulled on her handbrake and sat several minutes looking at the tall yellowish grass in the lights from her car. Then she got out and stood a moment, holding the paper bag at her side, before starting slowly through the damp grass along a narrow, overgrown path.

She stumbled once on a rock, but caught her balance and continued on till a dim square of light appeared ahead. Stopping, she looked at the outline of a window, part of it hidden behind the branch of a tree. Faintly she heard the sound of a man's voice. She walked forward, a bush scraping her arm as she reached a small clearing. From its edge she could see through the window more clearly.

Standing at the stove in a long green robe was Paul. Laura watched as he looked down at a book open in front of him, beside one of the burners. He lifted the lid off a pan and stirred something in it several times. "I'm ready for you to chop the egg now, John," he said, replacing the lid. He looked back at the book as the door opened behind him.

Laura watched as her husband stepped into the kitchen.

"It's on the counter."

John went to a small bowl and lifted out an egg.

"Sit down at the table," Paul said, "and take your time peeling it. I don't want it getting all crappy the way it does when you're not careful."

John carried the egg to a table. "What are we making," he said, "Russian salad dressing?"

Paul turned a page of the book. "The Russian dressing you're used to is dyed mayonnaise. This originated with the czars."

Laura turned and walked through the wet grass to the side of the house. A large leaf from a banana tree hung down across a door. She glanced again across the yard. Inside the kitchen, Paul had gone to the sink. Laura placed her hand on the knob of the door. Holding the large cold leaf out of the way, she opened the door and stepped into the house.

Across the room a statue of a dog rested on top of a large television set. Laura stood looking at it a few moments, then glanced down at a low table beside her. On it was a book, and next to it a small plastic box. She reached for it. Turning it over, she saw several buttons and a dial. She squinted at them in the dim light, then glanced at the television again. She felt along the row of buttons in her hand to the one on top. Resting her thumb on it, she looked toward the kitchen door. Slowly she pressed down on the button till she heard a click. Suddenly the room was filled with bluish light. On the television screen was the picture of a man at a podium, while from the speaker beneath him came the sound of his voice. Laura placed the box down on the table and walked into a small room several yards away.

The kitchen door opened. Paul looked out. "Who left that on," he said.

John leaned to one side to see past him to the television set. "You must have."

"I never touched it."

The sandals Paul was wearing made a soft slapping noise against his heels as he walked into the living room. "It's the president," he said, bending down to pick up the box on the table, "shall we watch?"

John continued looking through the door of the kitchen, a half-cut hardboiled egg in his hand. "Turn it off, Paul."

There was a click as the screen went dark. Paul rested the switch on the table and walked back toward the kitchen. "You're slicing it too thick." He closed the door behind him.

Laura stood in the dark and listened. A faucet was turned on, then off. By the light shining across the back yard from the kitchen window she could see a broken chair lying on its side in the grass. She took a step toward the table in the living room again, waiting a moment as one of the men coughed on the other side of the door. Then she reached for the box, which was now resting partially on the book. She felt across the top of it and then pushed several buttons. Again the picture of the president's face appeared on the screen as his voice filled the room. She put the box down on the book again and stepped back out of sight.

The kitchen door opened and Paul walked out. "Is somebody here?" he said, looking in the direction of the front door.

John came out of the kitchen.

"It's on again," Paul said, walking across the room to the television. "You don't suppose that cretin's gotten control of our TV sets."

"Pull the plug out," John said.

Paul got down on his knees beside the set. He reached around to remove the plug from the wall, then got to his feet and walked back across the room, following John through the doorway. "It never did that before."

Laura stepped into the living room and walked back to the television. Keeping her eyes on the door to the kitchen, she crouched and felt on the carpet behind the set till her hand touched a cord. She found the plug at the end, then raised it to the wall, moving her fingers back and forth over the plaster till the small openings of a socket came against her hand. She turned the tiny prongs of the plug around and jiggled them against the holes till they slid in. Light filled the room. She hurried to the set, turning a large dial as far as it would go. A vase began vibrating on a table beside the wall as the voice of the president poured out. She ran back through her door.

Paul hurried out of the kitchen and across the living room. He grabbed a handle extending out from the end of a metal sheath hanging above the fireplace and pulled out a long metal sword.

John stepped into the room. "You must not have unplugged it."

"Go call the police." Holding the sword in front of himself, Paul stepped away from the fireplace.

"You didn't unplug it."

"Don't stand there," he said loudly, turning toward the dining room, waving the sword through the air, "go to the phone!"

"God, Elsie," John said as he walked into the small dark room, "no one's going to break into your damn house to turn on your TV."

Standing behind the partially closed door, Laura watched him pull a tiny chain on a lamp. He reached for the phone. As he lifted the receiver, she stepped out from the wall. "Hello, John."

John turned toward her, his finger in the dial of the telephone.

"I'm here."

It was quiet a moment, then Paul's sandals slapped toward them. The door was pushed inward. Holding the sword at his side, he looked in at Laura. He turned to John. "John, I don't believe this." He looked at Laura again. "They told me at the clinic I wouldn't have nightmares anymore."

"You're awake, Paul." She held out the paper bag. "The boy at the store sends his regrets."

"How did you get here," John said.

"I'm not here to talk about how I found you."

"It wasn't me, John," Paul said, raising his right hand. "On my mother's eyes it wasn't." He removed the paper bag from her hand. "John, it wasn't." He lifted the bottle out of the bag. "She brought our brandy," he said. "John, we can have our drinks now." He rested the sword in a corner.

"Not till I know how she got here."

Paul rested his hand on John's sleeve. "Let's just say there will be a certain party to whom I'll be very interested in talking upon his return from South America."

"Thomas?"

"Just leave Thomas to me."

"I came here to talk to you, John."

"I don't care why you came here. You're going out the way you came."

"It's not that simple, John."

Paul untwisted the cap of the bottle and sniffed it. "This is the stuff, John."

"You want to talk to me, Laura? You be at Roger's and my office tomorrow morning."

She shook her head.

"Don't you push me," he said.

Paul began tugging at his sleeve. "We can have our Boris Godunovs, John."

"Eleven at the office or nothing. You decide." John and Paul began walking through the living room.

"Half of this and half vodka," Paul said as they went into the kitchen, "we'll both be upside down after three of them." He closed the door.

For several moments Laura stood looking across the room. From the kitchen came the sound of a chair scraping over the floor. She walked to the door and opened it. "You can't ignore me away, John."

He looked up from his chair. "I told you to go."

Paul carried a small glass of purplish liquid toward her and held it out. "See if this doesn't bring out your better qualities."

She went to the table. "I will be treated fairly, John."

"Tomorrow at the office."

"Do you think I'm walking out of here after what I've been through." She seated herself at the table. "Do you really believe a few harsh words from you are going to make me turn and run after what's happened."

"She's angling for an invitation," Paul said. "Let's give her the room off the pantry."

Laura turned to look at him. "Do you think you could stay out of this."

Paul snapped his fingers. "Laura, you aren't going to believe this, but there's a lady's nightgown in the next room and I'll bet you a hairpin it's just your size. Don't you move now." He walked through the door leading to the back.

"What is he doing."

"He wants you to stay over," John said. "I guess it seems peculiar to him not to have the two of you spending the night under the same roof."

"And what does that mean."

Holding a long white negligee trimmed with feathers, Paul returned to the room. "Before you say no, I just want to hold it up one second for fit." He took the back of her chair. "Up you get."

"She's not staying," John said.

Paul began rocking the chair. "We'll pull out the cerise ribbon in the bodice if it doesn't compliment your natural highlights, but just so I can see how we are for length why don't you stand up tall while I measure." He rocked the chair several more times, then pulled it back hard.

Laura grabbed the sides of the table to keep from falling.

"Sorry about that. Now just get up and let Paul hold it up, because there's nothing worse than a nightie that bothers our little footsies while we're trying to get to sleep."

Laura rose from the table, grabbed the gown out of his hand, and let it drop to the linoleum floor.

"You don't like it."

"I'll say one thing to you," she said softly. "Then I want to be alone with John."

Paul bent over to pick it up. "Would it make a difference if you knew it was worn by Joan Crawford in *Horror Street* in 1962?"

"Paul, there's no way for you and I to understand each other."

"It's the feathers, isn't it."

"You have done something," Laura said, "that was wrong. And I don't want you to think I'm passing judgment on you, but I'm asking you not to speak to me again." She walked back to the table.

"Just one last interruption." Paul went to the stove.

"John, I want you to go into the next room with me."

"Laura, either you're very dumb, or your mental condition has deteriorated seriously since the last time we spoke. You're not wanted here."

"I think that's clear enough, John."

"We're making Russian cheesecake." Paul fitted a large quilted glove onto his hand. "Only it's begun to look awfully orangy to me." He pulled open the oven door. "Would you two mind taking a peek?"

"I need to know, John, if you think he and I went to bed together."

"You can forget about my offer to meet privately with you, Laura. The only circumstances in which I will now meet with you are at the office of my lawyer. You have his address."

"Tell me if you think I went to bed with this person, John."

John pushed his chair back and stood.

"If you need it to be said that I don't jump into bed with persons other than you at the drop of a hat, John, then I'll say it. That I went to bed with this man is the most preposterous and absurd nonsense."

"Laura," Paul said, "did you ever see the uncut version of *Indiscretion?*"

She turned toward him. "So far, Paul, I have taken great care to express myself in a way which is not altogether consistent with the extent of my emotional feelings toward the person in whose presence John and I find ourselves."

"Just come out and say you're talking about me, Laura. There's no beating around the bush in this house."

"Is that right."

"House rule number four."

"Well that's good to know, Paul. If there's no beating around the bush here, why don't you tell my husband, in front of me, that you and I had sexual relations with each other in a motel in Santa Barbara. Go ahead and say it to his face while I'm standing here."

"Say John," Paul said, walking across the room, "this little lady has more spunk than we've given her credit for. What do you say we take her on."

"Laura's going home now." John turned to his wife. "We'll meet tomorrow at Washington's office. If you have a lawyer, bring him."

"You're both being silly," Paul said. "I'm offering her a place here. John, we can use her."

"Come on, Paul."

"You think I'm joking? She can move in tonight and tomorrow we'll all go up and help her bring her things. No enormous duties for her. A little shopping in the morning. Possibly some light gardening in the afternoon. An hour or two on the beach after the midday sun has passed. What more could any girl ask?"

"Go home, Laura," John said.

"John, how can you even spend five minutes in the same room with this person."

"I'll even let her hang my Cornel Wilde breastplate on her wall. Wait a minute." Paul held up his hands. "Wait a minute. The perfect solution, John, to all our problems. She can be nanny for the children."

Laura turned quickly toward him.

"She's had an earlier relationship with them. She's familiar with their habits. They'll get along famously."

"Do I understand what you're saying," Laura said.

"John, it's too perfect."

"Are you talking about John's and my children."

"Just this morning, John, you were saying there was going to be a problem with your writing after the children came." He gestured at Laura. "*Voilà.*"

"That's enough, Paul," John said.

Laura turned to her husband. "All right, John."

"Who played that glorious domestic in the television remake of *Cheaper by the Dozen?*"

"John, your friend Paul has perjured himself to a court of law. Do you understand that."

"I will not get into any of this with you now, Laura."

"Well you will get into it because I don't think you do understand it." She pointed at Paul. "He has made a sworn statement, knowing it was false, lying under oath to a representative of the court in writing. There's no way for him to deny it. The result of his lie, saying that he and I went to bed together, was a court order, carried out this afternoon, by which your children, Tommy and Flora Foster, were separated from their legal mother. And if you were knowingly involved in what he's done, John, if you took part in his setting up the appointment at the studio with Mr. Washington where he signed the paper, if you were aware he was doing it and let him go ahead, you may be subject to jail."

"Laura, if you insist, this will be the subject of the meeting tomorrow."

"This isn't a subject, John. These are our children. And I'm going to get them back tomorrow. I'm going to Mr. Washington, and to the judge. I'm not wasting time getting a lawyer. I'm simply going to whoever I have to and tell the truth, that I tracked you down. That I came out here to find the two of you baking Russian cheesecake and making jokes about my being your governess."

John glanced at Paul.

"I don't know your motives in this," she said, turning to Paul, "and I don't care. Earlier today you were talking about my leading you on. If I wronged you somehow, I apologize. But my children are staying away from me tonight in a state home and you're responsible. And you're going to pay for it." She took a step toward him. "You're going to pay dearly, and if you think this whole thing is funny, then you get all the laughs you can out of it in a hurry."

Paul looked over at John. "A wrath scene," he said.

"No, this is not a wrath scene," she said. "It's the judge who's going to have the wrath scene."

"Laura, Paul told me two hours ago it wasn't true about Santa Barbara. I plan to take it up with Washington in the morning."

"You plan to tell Washington he was lying."

"I plan to tell him Paul's a homosexual and that he wasn't positive there had been penetration."

"I wasn't." Paul shrugged.

She turned to look at him. "You were in a bed with a space of four feet between the bed of another person and you're not sure if what my husband refers to as penetration occurred."

"I will work this out with Mr. Washington, Laura," John said.

"I wonder if it will please Mr. Washington to learn that by taking you on as a client it's put him in a position of making false statements to a court. I rather doubt it, John."

"If it helps," he said, "at the time the court took them away this afternoon, I believed you had slept with Paul."

"It doesn't." Again she pointed at Paul. "Because now that you know I didn't, you still stand there and defend this person. Knowing that he lied to you, and caused this misery to your children."

Paul removed his quilted glove and set it on the stove.

"I don't approve of what he did," John said.

"You don't."

"No."

"Well that's pretty strong. Someone lies to you about sleeping with your wife. He deprives your children of their home. And you disapprove."

"I'll see that Tommy and Flora are returned to you tomorrow."

"I will expect that."

"But I'm going to do it in a way that Paul doesn't get hurt."

"John, he's going to get the book thrown at him."

"He's sorry for what he did, Laura," John said, looking at Paul. "He did it because you wronged him."

"I didn't wrong him."

"It was your idea to go up there with him. You went voluntarily to the motel with him. This led to certain things being in his mind. Your actions put them there."

"John, it sounds as though you would have preferred me to go to bed with him."

"You led him on, Laura."

She held up her hand. "All right, John. If you really think there's a way to get Tommy and Flora back without him getting what he deserves, I guess that's your business."

"I don't believe, Laura," Paul said, walking to the cupboard to remove a set of carved wooden salt and pepper shakers, "as many of my colleagues do, that members of your sex are by nature vindictive. But I would be less than honest not to say your remarks here tonight are straining my credibility on the subject." He set the salt and pepper shakers on the table and picked up his drink. "Excuse me."

Laura watched him walk out of the room, listening till the sound of his sandals died away before turning back to her husband.

"You've upset him," John said.

"Oh, dear."

"You've come into his house, insulted him, and hurt him. Now I'm going to say something that will seem very abrupt to you. I'll say it just once." He cleared his throat softly.

"May I say why I hurt him?"

"When I leave this room," he said, "if you follow me, I will not be responsible for what I do to you physically. What happens will be your fault, if you come after me." He looked up at her. "Laura, I would rather spend the rest of my life locked up than five more minutes of it with you."

She was standing in the same place, still looking through the doorway into the next room, when Paul returned. He set his empty glass in the sink and replaced the large glove on his hand. Then he opened the door of the oven. "Our main course tonight, Laura." he said, pulling a green casserole dish out of the stove, "is Cutlets Kiev, or, as it's more popularly called, simply Chicken Kiev."

She watched him place the dish on top of the stove.

"Its name derives from a city in the Ukraine." He removed the lid from the pan on the rear burner. "It may come as a surprise, Laura, to learn that one need not be of a particular national origin to partake and enjoy that country's cuisine." He removed two plates from a cupboard and set them side by side on the stove. "Obviously the best way to experience foreign dishes is by traveling in the country itself." He took down a large spoon hanging on a leather cord behind the stove and heaped two piles of rice onto the plates. "But in your case a Russian trip would be highly unadvisable until the Colonel Sanders chain is well established throughout the Black Sea region." Using the spoon, he carefully lifted a brownish ball out of the casserole dish. He placed it on a pile of rice, then began moving the spoon back for the second one.

"John doesn't even like chicken," Laura said.

"What is it?" he said, glancing at her.

"He doesn't like it. He never has."

"I'm sure it depends upon how it's prepared."

"It makes no difference."

Suddenly Paul dropped the spoon on the stove and pulled back his arm. He rubbed his hand against the sleeve of his robe, then looked down at a red mark across the back of his fingers. "Get me an ice cube." He raised his hand to his mouth, sucked on it a moment, then lowered it again. "Do you suppose after all the disruption you've brought here you could at least walk across the room for an ice cube?"

She was gone.

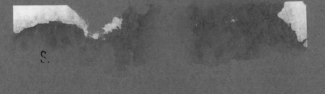